Ghosts and Things

Richard Small

Edward Gaskell
Devon

Edward Gaskell publishers
Park Cottage
Grange Road
Bideford
Devon
EX39 4AS

First published 2015

Front cover photo:
St John the Baptist Church,
Countisbury, North Devon

ISBN 978-1-906769-63-5

Ghosts and Things

Richard Small

Typeset, printed and bound by
Lazarus Press
6 Grenville Street
Bideford
Devon
EX39 3DX
www.lazaruspress.com

DEDICATION

This book is dedicated to the seeker within you
and to all our absent friends. Like memories and the
ghosts of story, they still remain with us in spirit.

My special thanks and enduring love go to
Jocelyn and Samuel, whose very presence
on this Earth encourages me to achieve.

You may contact the author via www.goodshortstories.net

*"If you will believe in me then I will believe in you," whispered the
Unicorn from mythical pastures beyond the fence we cannot see.*

ABOUT THE AUTHOR.

Richard John Small was born in 1948 in the once industrial town of Bedford on the site where his great, great, grandfather had died a workhouse pauper in 1885. Richard grew up in a gardenless Victorian terraced house. He attended the same school buildings as had his grandmother before him, and with the exception of one truly brilliant English teacher, Richard's education and learning was never much to write home about.

Coloured by the dust of his road - as we all cannot help but be - and after a few lazy years, he was driven by a need to prove himself adequate in life. In pursuit of some sense of worthiness and seeking to be valued by others he engaged in various activities like pot holing and extreme walks (the 40 miles of the Lyke Wake). He climbed Ben Nevis, Snowdon, Helvellyn, and took up martial arts, eventually being awarded 4th Dan black belt in Aikido. In an often failing attempt to improve his lot and that of his family he sought qualifications, enough to wallpaper a small room. . . HNC Chemistry, BTEC Fire Command and Management Studies, Post Grad Diploma in Training, UK Fire Engineering Diploma. He was a Graduate of the Institution of Fire Engineers for over 30 years and for several years was a Chartered Member of the Institute of Personnel and Development. The desire for worthy knowledge and skills led to an even greater desire to share the same, to make life easier for those following. Richard held instructor qualifications in further and adult education, RYA power boat and RYA first aid, and within the fire and rescue service he was a Breathing Apparatus and a Road Traffic Accident instructor as well as Radiation and Hazardous materials officer. He became a qualified coach in the Chinese art of Tai Chi and travelled many times to China and Russia in pursuit of martial arts.

The list goes on. One minute he was a valuable resource and the next ostensibly useless. . . that's what retirement seems to offer many in this life.

Now retired to the land of his well researched ancestors he spends a good measure of his time writing short stories and contributing to various publications, practising his martial arts and walking in the beautiful countryside of Devon and Cornwall. In the past and as today he would also seek out the quiet spiritual retreats. A one time student of NLP he remains a student of his own mind, forever looking for doorways that open up to new understandings. No stranger to the alternative therapies like Reiki nor to meditation and Chi Kung, blood donor, Greenpeace supporter, chickens hatched, gardens dug, bodies buried and pianos moved and all round not a bad bloke at all (so he says with a smile and a touch of humility) he philosophically offers you these short tales of the supernatural.

How much truth is hidden within these tales is for you to decide.

Late one dark and lonely evening, if you find an elderly lady in Victorian garb standing in your dimly lit hallway and deep within you know she has been dead for over a hundred and forty years, it will make you think. . . it certainly did him!

"When I let go of who I am. . . I become who I might be."

Lao Tzu

By the same author

I Want to Tell You a Story. . .
First published 2012
Reprinted March 2013
ISBN 978-1-906769-35-2
Edward Gaskell
Publishers
DEVON

Contact the author direct via
www.goodshortstories.net

Contents

Foreword and ethos of the book.

The author invites you to step quietly from your everyday world into a different reality. And to sit a while with these inspiring tales, drawn inexorably from an ancient land of deep wooded combes, wild moors and highwaymen. A land of rugged coasts and wreckers, a place where you will never be sure if it's the gulls or the souls of long wrecked sailors that you hear cry out in the storm.

Pried open for you from the stuff of life and its beyond, these entertaining tales create an inviting portal that allows your soul safe passage to discover what is on the other side. Through the time-honoured gift of story and steeped in the essence of the supernatural, these twenty six simple tales of ghosts and things will disclose normally elusive insights about supernatural phenomena.

We all know that the boundaries between adventure, caution and the supernatural are often blurred but here both writer and reader can cross that exciting line to other worlds. The seeker within you will surely find meaningful and profound wisdoms, insights, messages and answers - and the author has no doubt that you will bump into yourself as you explore this 'no man's land.'

> *'No tears in the writer, no tears in the reader.*
> *No surprise in the writer, no surprise in the reader.'*
> Robert Frost.

We are none of us strangers to the tears or surprises of which Frost wrote and which populate life's intriguing journey. If something from beyond the conscious mind has penned these pages then your soul will be the judge.

Look no further, wait no longer, for the guide awaits you at an open door.

"Footfalls echo in the memory,
down the passage we did not take,
towards the door we never opened,
into the rose garden."

T S Eliot

FREMINGTON QUAY
THE YOUNG MARINER'S RETURN.
(A family oriented short tale of the supernatural)

It all began, not that many years gone by, with the Richmond family's holiday disaster (that being Mrs Richmond's final and considered opinion on the matter). Life would never be the same again, not after that holiday!

*

'Cycling and camping - you just can't beat it,' beamed a contented Dave Richmond to himself as he dragged his reluctant family along the Tarka trail from Barnstaple. He paused for a while to catch his breath and sensed the promise of a cool September evening mist drawing ever closer. Closer too came his distraught wife and highly agitated children, as they pedalled hard to catch him up.

'Why on earth couldn't we have taken a B&B in town?' pleaded his wife Caroline, gasping for breath. The two, temporarily mum-supportive girls, Lucy 12 and Lizbeth 9 enthusiastically agreed.

Dave ignored their reluctance to continue, 'Are we men or mice, eh? When I was in the boy scouts we did this all the time. You'll love it! Trust me. Just up ahead is a quaint and historic place called Fremington Quay. I'll treat you all to a warm meal at the café. . . come on. . . last one there's a big sissy.'

With that he was gone, pedalling as fast as he could go.

There were however a number of relevant considerations that Dave hadn't fully grasped. One, the girls weren't, nor ever would be, boy scouts. Two, the café was not only closed but was also temporarily deserted. Three, time had given him a rose-tinted and favourably distorted view of the dubious pleasures of autumnal camping.

As Dave approached the deserted Quay, his heart sank; he could plainly see the café was closed, with not a single living soul in sight. What would his family say? He resolved to put on a brave face and pretend it was all part of his plan, the great adventure. 'The rich tapestry of life itself,' he'd tell them.

'We'll camp here tonight,' he said pointing to a flat grassed area close by the now full River Taw; it wasn't so far off high water slack and the nearby long-drowned mud banks lay patiently waiting for the ebb tide so they would see light and breathe air once again.

There were lots of moans and groans but they had little choice, for both night and river mist had arrived and they didn't know where else they could go. Dave did of course. . . But 'defeat' wasn't an option. As leader of the family he had a face to save. . . his own!

This was one decision that would prove to haunt the family for longer than they could possibly imagine.

Their two tents were soon pitched and the little camping gas burner warmed their hands as well as some reserve soup rations. The family didn't stay long outside. Despite it being early, the penetrating dark cold of the river mist forced them to retreat to the sleeping bag warmth of their tents.

'Not too long with those little lamps, girls! Those batteries must last you all week. We didn't have such luxuries in the boy scouts you know. . . Night, night, sleep well,' advised Dave, his voice somewhat muffled by his own sleeping bag. The girls just about heard their mother asking if he'd also worn that silly woolly hat to bed in the boy scouts. They giggled a little at the thought and then lay there chatting very quietly with their lamps on, obscured from parental eyes by their sleeping bags. Eventually Lizbeth fell asleep but Lucy was lying on lumpy ground that felt more like stones than grass; move as she might it was difficult to be comfortable. Insomnia and the cold kept her fitfully awake for a couple of hours listening to the sound of her sister's breathing, the occasional snore from the neighbouring tent and the silence, the otherwise total silence. It was the silence she could hear more than anything.

Then she heard it. . . a far off creaking noise from the direction of the river. Now she was eyes-staring wide awake, she fumbled for her little torch. Oh no! She'd left it switched on by mistake and now its life hung on by the faintest orange glimmer. She could hear splashing in the river nearby, accompanied by a sort of knocking noise; she stopped breathing to hear it the better. Then there was silence again. By now she was too frightened to make a single sound; Lucy began to sense a presence beyond the tent, an invisible presence that was able to pass through the tent fabric and then, the strangest of feelings. It was most peculiar, like putting her feet in a lukewarm bath but from the inside. The unstoppable feeling slowly completed its journey to the top of her head. Nothing bad was happening, she felt fine, it was just an odd feeling that she soon seemed to get used to. After about an hour of wakefulness and puzzlement Lucy drifted off, at times she even felt like she was being rocked gently to sleep.

Morning came with the sound of agitated dog walkers calling their dogs away from scent marking the family tents. Dave was first up, complete with woolly hat and a determination to lead the way again. He put the kettle on the burner and went across the heavily dewed grass to investigate the boarded up and now obviously deserted café in daylight. By the time he returned, Caroline had already made some hot drinks and was chatting to a shivering Lizbeth. 'And where's Lucy then?' he asked, 'We didn't get to lie in when we were in the boy scouts you know.'

He was cut short by a stern, uncompromising look from his wife, 'She's not feeling too well, had an awful night's sleep, bad dreams and all that, just not herself today. . . I told you we should have gone B&B. Why not listen for once?' scolded Caroline, thinking it was a pity that the boy scouts hadn't bestowed her husband with the benefit of a bit more common sense.

Their holiday was cut short and they went home and back to normal, everyone that is, except Lucy. Lucy didn't eat too well, lost concentration easily and spent most of her time talking about the strange dreams she was having, dreams of being places she had never heard of - never mind visited; dreams where she felt pain, cold and loneliness; dreams that came leaving Lucy gasping for breath and in a state of blind panic calling for her mother in the dark.

Of course Caroline took her to the doctors but they didn't have any idea what to do. If anything they were all at sea with not knowing what to do, their advice being just the usual stuff that might with luck fit something they didn't understand. Then one day the family doctor suggested seeing a psychiatrist. 'Stone the crows,' Dave whispered to his wife, 'do they think she's gone mad? Why see this psycho whatever person? She'll be fine, just needs a bit more time that's all.' But time wasn't going to change anything, Lucy continued to have the dreams and the dreams continued to be the unhappy same.

A month later they were visiting the outpatients department at the nearest Psychiatric Unit and seeing a really kind young lady who spent an hour or so chatting to Lucy. As Lucy and her dad walked to the car discussing the 'nice lady,' Caroline was being given a findings report and most-likely conjecture on Lucy's problem. 'Well she's a lovely little girl, seems quite normal to me, I think we can put it down to an over-active imagination coupled with the trauma of camping out in the cold and damp against her wishes. I suspect it's a subconscious rebellion thing. I'm sure she'll be fine, just give it a bit more time. . . perhaps take her out in the sunshine to a park or boating lake or something similar. So glad to have been of help; always feel free to call on us again, bye, bye Mrs Richmond.'

Caroline was not the least bit impressed with the system's tardy, so-called 'help' but did however take the girls out to the park for a picnic in the sunshine. While they were all enjoying the little treats Caroline had provided, Lucy suddenly went white and almost stopped breathing. . . 'What's wrong?' panicked Caroline. 'What is the matter Lucy?'

Lucy took a gasp of breath, 'That noise, mum, that's the noise, the one I heard at the Quay that night, that clonk, clonk noise. Just like that it was, then it went quiet.'

'Oh, Lucy, look, it's just someone in a rowing boat; it's the noise the oars make against the boat, see, look, 'splash, clonk, clonk,' it's just a rowing boat that's all,' assured her mother. Sadly by then the mood had changed for the worse and the family returned home. Caroline was at her wits end to help her daughter and was telephoning a good friend about her woes when her friend made a strange suggestion, 'I know a medium,' she said, a really good one, no mumbo jumbo stuff, really good. I can ask for you if you like.'

'I'll check with Dave first, I doubt he'll go for something like that, he's always ridiculed such things in the past; I'll check with him and get back to you. Thank you though for your kindly support,' Caroline said, thoughtfully replacing the receiver very slowly.

As it happened and to Caroline's great surprise Dave was all for it. 'We must help the poor girl, even if it *is* mumbo jumbo as long as it works then, who cares? All we want is to have our daughter back - back home with us from wherever her mind has gone. Phone them back; we'll give it a try.'

She gave him a hug, 'thank you, thank you, I'll phone her right away.'

**

The evening of the 'medium' arrived, as did the medium herself, a dear little old lady called Hilda. Hilda had lots of grandchildren of her own and was soon at one with the girls, they seemed to warm to her immediately.

'Going well so far,' whispered Dave to his wife.

'Shhshh dear, let's not speak unless asked,' she replied.

Hilda and Lucy sat close together on the bottom two steps of the stairwell while the rest of the family sat on the carpeted hallway floor, leaned against the walls and listened intently.

In a soft comforting voice, Hilda began, 'Well, Lucy, I hear you have been having some strange dreams that don't really fit your own experiences in life. I'll tell you a secret, just between me and you - it's because sometimes they are not just our *own* dreams but sometimes they belong to someone else. I think I can tell you about the 'someone else' in your case and how we can get them to stop. It is a boy, not much older than you and he is a lost soul. He needs our help to get home - we can help him quite easily. What do you say? Shall we have a go?'

Lucy nodded with a smile; she felt empowered by Hilda's presence and was beginning to feel more in control of her fears. Intuitively, Hilda picked up on Lucy's unspoken feeling and agreed, 'Yes Lucy, a fear, once it's understood, no longer frightens us. Strange isn't it?'

'Okay, dear, I'll tell you what I know and you just stop me at any time to add something or ask a question, alright, my lovely? We are going back in time, to the birth of this boy to a poor family - it is 1836, at a place, you probably never heard of, Fremington Quay. . .'

Lucy interrupted excitedly, 'I know it! I know it! That's where we went on holiday and where the dreams started. . .' Hilda smiled; she now knew for sure she was on the right track.

'I see a young boy growing up,' Hilda continued. 'A name is coming to me. . . Leonard. Leonard. . .'

'Goulde!' interrupted Lucy excitedly. 'I don't know how I know - it just came into my mind, just now.'

'Yes,' said Hilda, 'you are right. Leonard Goulde he is indeed. When he was only twelve years of age, reluctantly he had to be sent away to sea by his father who could no longer afford to feed him. I sense the sobbing heartache of his mother. A couple of years later his ship returned to the Quay and without seeking permission Leonard took the ship's small boat and rowed ashore in the mist to find his family. They were not there. They were nowhere to be seen, he looked and looked but could not find them. He searched for so long that by then the mist-hidden ebb of the tide was at its peak; Leonard's strength and the little boat were no match for the current as he desperately tried to reach his ship. Well the sad thing is, with the ebbing current so powerful, he drowned. We can't change that, it's what happened and it might explain why you have held your breath at times when his presence was close. Anyway, ever since then on certain September nights when the mist and the tide are as they were on his final and fateful night, Leonard returns, still searching for his beloved family. Unless we help him, he will search forever.' Hilda paused. 'Are you still okay with this Lucy?'

Lucy nodded enthusiastically, this was the first time anybody had understood what she was experiencing and she felt completely safe with Hilda.

'I think,' confided Hilda to Lucy, 'that the cold, the fear and your need for home that night, coincided with the very feelings Leonard experienced and that 'fear' connected the dead with the living. . . through a sort of gateway. We can re-open that gate and set him free too. I have an idea.'

Looking up at Caroline, who was watching spellbound by the revelations, Hilda suggested, 'Tomorrow, after school, let the three of us go to the records office in Barnstaple town and see if we can find our Leonard. We might also find our answer there.'

'Yes,' added Lucy, 'poor Leonard will never find his family with me, he needs to go back home to find them.'

**

The next day they met at the records office; kindly staff brought them the documents they needed and recommended they try the 1841 Census first.

Looking through the pages, Hilda found a Goulde, Leonard. 'Here he is - it says aged five,' she said pointing, 'and, here, look, his father, a William Goulde, coal porter.'

Lucy reached out and placed her finger on the name below, 'Mother,' she said in a soft voice that intimated a long awaited reunion. Poignancy not lost on Hilda but she knew when to say nothing.

The archivists advised they try the 1851 census and produced the Fremington Quay documents, But no Goulde family was recorded as living there in that year. They searched in vain, as too had young Leonard on that desperate night. 'Oh, that poor boy,' sighed Hilda. 'It looks like when he returned from sea they weren't there; poor child, so young to be away from his family. Life was much harder for everyone then for sure.'

'They could have moved any time after 1841,' staff suggested. 'You could look for baptisms for other children but that would take some time. Let's look in the index for Goulde in other parishes for the 1851 census.'

There were a couple of possible references but one in particular stood out. 'There he is!' said a staff member. 'Look. Here, William Goulde, still working as a coal porter and living in Pilton down by the Yeo Quayside. And it looks like the family have two more children by this time too.'

Lucy peered closer at the page, 'Yes, oh yes! This is my family,' not realising what she was saying, but Hilda knew and hid a smile. 'This is them!'

As they walked to the car park, Hilda gave Lucy a hug around the shoulders. 'You don't need me any more dear, what you need to do is to return with your family to Fremington Quay one misty evening when the tide is as it was the night you camped and the gateway will be open for Leonard to go home again. Now we have shown him where to find his mother he can make his own way. You can feel proud of yourself; you have saved a desperate and lonely soul from his never ending search which trapped him in another place and time. I am so proud of you. Well done - now I must also say goodbye. We'll not forget each other, will we?'

Lucy gave Hilda a big hug and thanked her for saving 'her own soul,' as she put it. Hilda got into the little car that was waiting for her with her husband, Fred, and with a final wave, was gone.

**

It had been a year of mystifying hell but all seemed worthwhile now they understood. The family drove one misty afternoon to the Quay café to follow Hilda's instructions. The café was quiet, only the owners present; The Richmonds enjoyed hot drinks and home made cake and were made most welcome. As the family shared their secret and their troubles into the early evening, the young owner and his wife kept open as if they had invited friends and family in their company.

After a couple of hours Lucy rose calmly and said, 'I'm just going for a little walk, I won't be going far.'

Dave wanted to go with her or at least wanted to tell her to keep away from the edge but something inside him told him to be quiet and that all would be well. There is a time to trust.

Lucy, now almost spirit like herself, walked slowly in the sea mist, across the heavily dewed grass towards the river. As she came to the railings she stopped and whispered, 'Goodbye Leonard, safe journey, say hello to your mum for me. I'm sure she waited everyday for you to come home. God bless, bye, bye.' Lucy sensed that she was now standing all alone; alone with a tear in her eye, a tear of happiness for Leonard whose soul she had touched and he hers. Only Lucy's ears that night would hear the splash of water and the clonk, clonk of ghostly oars in rowlocks. Invisible in the September mist, a little boat was eagerly being rowed up river on a flowing tide towards Pilton's Yeo Quay and the peace of coming home at last.

'Night has brought to those who sleep only dreams they cannot keep.'

Enya.

Lucy, with serenity beyond her years, stood a moment or two, surrounded by a peace of her own, then returned to her family in the café.

'Time to go home now mum, just the four of us this time,' exclaimed a beaming Lucy standing in the doorway.

Life could never be the same again. . . it could only be better.

'Wisdom and compassion are the best of companions.'

CHILDREN OF THE GINGERBREAD HOUSE.

(Another family 'ghost' story filled with puns about knitting. Based on real events and people).

The time to leave was looming ever closer for Dave, who had hoped for a very different Saturday indeed. 'Right, come on kids, get a move on, toys in the box, we're off to some old knitting exhibition your mum wants to see,' said father of two Dave, as he jingled his car keys impatiently in his hand. Dave shouted up the stairs for his wife Becky, 'Come on dear, we're all ready to go. . . your mum's here too.' Dave raised his eyes slightly to the heavens. Why his wife was never ready or why she'd invited her mum to this 'knitting thing,' he'd never understand. 'What is it with knitting anyway?' He thought deeply to himself.

Becky's voice from outside the open front doorway suddenly brought him back from his pensive state. 'Come on then you woolly headed nit wit, let's be having you, you're always last,' she said in a happy, joking manner.

Presently, they were all neatly strapped into their seats in the family car and safely on their way with Dave at the wheel, Becky beside him with the exhibition brochure and squeezed between the two child seats at the back, his mother-in-law, Hannah.

Katie was four and a half and Luke, three and a half. . . both had wild imaginations; Too wild sometimes for Dave, who was more down to earth about most things – okay, everything.

On arrival at the exhibition hall, by sheer luck they found one parking space left. With the children already made increasingly hyper by their grandmother's tales and over liberal sweetie hand outs, Dave said, 'Okay, Becky, I'll wait here I think, how long will you be?'

Becky gave him an icily derisory look that made it quite clear that he was joining them inside and would be enjoying it, regardless.

They were all welcomed into the hall by a nice lady called Alison who told the children they too could knit something if they wished, but the children only had eyes for a little house made of wool. Alison felt their excitement at seeing the gingerbread house and summoned a volunteer over to show them around. 'You can call me Sean,' he said with a big friendly smile as he led them closer to the biggest 'doll's house' Katie had ever seen. Even Dave was impressed- and not much in life did that.

The adults marvelled at the knitting prowess and constructive imagination of the builders of the Gingerbread house and Sean explained some of the features in depth, 'it is also filled with wonders from the world of wool and knitters,' he said. 'The original didn't have a fence but we added that and the gate to keep the public out. . . people tried to rearrange the furniture to their own liking, children were put to bed in there so the parents could wander off for some peace, we had to vacuum picnic crumbs out of it and once found a homeless chap had moved in.' 'Anyway,' said Sean, who could obviously spin a good yarn, 'just touch some of the items in the garden; have an open mind and just reach over the fence. . . touch a flower.' As they obliged him by doing so, he continued, 'There, can you feel it? Can you sense the sort of person who knitted that piece, ask yourself; was it an old lady or a child?'

Dave admitted he could feel nothing, Becky thought perhaps she could but was a bit reluctant to commit to an answer for fear of being wrong. However, Hannah was well into this 'game' and flitted from item to item proclaiming with utter confidence who might have knitted what and even where.

Suddenly Becky issued a shrieking and blunt command to the children, 'Stop! You two, you stop right there, now come on out of the garden.'

By now, Katie and Luke were up to the front door of the Gingerbread house. 'It's okay lady, don't worry, they're safe there,' assured Sean. Becky wasn't thinking of their safety, she was thinking of how much damage they might do to the contents of this beautifully presented monument to the skills of countless knitters across the world.

Sean reassured Becky once again, 'Look, we don't normally do this, but you're lovely people and I can see the children want to see what treasures there may be inside. I'm only a stand-in guide while Colin is away looking at croft retreats in Shetland and knitting holidays in San Marino. It's very quiet at the moment and if you promise not to make it known to others, I'll take you inside. Sean's offer was met with three solemn nods in hushed and secret silence. Somehow Dave had found himself joining in, involuntarily. 'Weird that,' he thought.

They ducked their heads to enter in through the low door as the children pushed with strong hands past their legs to be in first. It was lighter inside than they thought it would be and immediately felt comfortably homely. As Becky and her mum gazed in wonder on row upon row of intricately knitted objects on knitted shelves, Dave was looking in horror, as though someone had sat on it, at a big dent in the otherwise beautifully made up bed, 'What have you done to the bed kids? You're not to climb on things, for Pete's sake do not touch stuff.'

'It wasn't us,' protested a very defensive Katie, 'it's a nice old lady knitting, and she's got a pet sheep called Barbara.'

At this point Dave gave up, the children were living in a different world to him and he certainly wasn't going to encourage them by continuing the conversation, 'Well don't touch things again, okay?'

Katie and Luke weren't even listening by now as they stroked Barbara's lovely clean fleece. Barbara even told them of her famous grandfather who had come from Ireland where the leprechauns live, his name was Lan O'Lin from County Scane and surely they must have had heard of him, why hundreds would flock to see him at the grand summer farm fairs. Barbara was obviously very proud of her lineage.

'We can knit Dave a cardigan, mum, couldn't we?' said Becky.

'We certainly could and it would be far nicer than some of those cast-off things he gets from the charity shop. There are some nice colours in here to choose from. Look Dave, what about this pink one,' smiled a cheekily knowing Hannah.

'You must be joking, I wouldn't be seen dead in that,' Dave retorted.

'You're wasting your time mum - casting pearls before swine,' Becky said, joining her mum with the joke.

'Sean,' said Hannah, 'should the house have been knitted with climbing plants on it?'

'What makes you ask that?' replied Sean, puzzled by the question.

'Well, you may think me strange but I keep hearing the word "Ivy" in my head, and I just wondered, that's all,' said Hannah, wishing she'd not said anything now.

'No, I'm not surprised because when I enter the gingerbread house I too hear things in my mind, I think it's like some energy left in the knitting, you know, the thoughts and feelings of the people who handled the wool and stuff. I'll ask Alison about Ivy later and see what she says,' assured Sean thoughtfully.

Dave's eyes rolled skywards again, he couldn't feel any 'energies' in the room except it was getting a little warm and his two children were all the energy he could cope with today anyway.

Katie and Luke ran about shrieking and laughing, they said they were chasing sheep. Dave turned to Becky, 'we need a sheep dog ourselves to keep control of these two, I think it's time we went home before they wreck the joint.'

'Mum, mum, can we take something with us, go on, please mum, go on mum. . . 'Katie and Luke chanted in that clever way that only children know.

Thinking what a smart move he'd made and that he'd out foxed them this time for sure, Dave told them, 'All right, all right, if you must, you can bring the little old knitting lady off the bed and her pet sheep Bobby if you must. . . '.

'Barbara, Dad, Barbara,' they shouted in unison.

After some brief but fond goodbyes to Sean and Alison their little car crunched across the gravel of the now empty car park and turned right for the road home.

'What a good day after all,' thought Dave. Becky was going to cook them all a special meal for teatime and he was going to be able to watch his favourite football match on the as yet unseen highlights programme; the day was fine and the family car was running beautifully too, all except for an intermittent click clack noise, which Dave soon dismissed and put down to a couple of stones in the tyres, probably picked up in the exhibition car park. Clutching her handbag on her lap, his mother-in-law was fast asleep between two excitedly chattering children. 'God only knows who they think they're talking to,' thought Dave, 'what wild imaginations they have for sure.'

**

'Our day is but a path we tread, a gentle path among possibilities.'

Kent Nerburn

MO'S DREAM.

Ithad been a tragic and frankly awful six months for Maureen, or Mo as her few close friends called her. Mo's mother had died suddenly and without any prior warning only the day before Mo and her agreeable husband, Alan, were to pay her a visit. Mo was a kindly lady in her early forties, same age as Alan, and the death of her mother at only sixty two, was an unwelcome and devastating shock.

Mo was a precious only child and her steadfastly protective mum had always looked out for her well-being until they'd moved many miles away for Alan to find better employment. The joy of visiting, laden with gifts, photos and news to share, took a crushing blow when the neighbours explained what had happened.

When they entered her mum's house it was neat and tidy, even more so than normal. The best china tea set was laid out ready on the polished front room table. Sharing the table was an old shoe box containing her mum's 'little treasures,' her grandmother's wedding ring, her father's military medals, lots of photos of Mo as a child and a miscellany of buttons, tickets and postcards. There too, lay a writing pad opened ready on the first page; alongside, a simple but pleasing silver fountain pen, a gift from Mo, with black ink and broad nib; however, the page was blank, not a mark, just blank. Alan and Mo often wondered what the empty page would have told them. If only they had gone the day before, if only her mum had written the note, if only, if only. . .

Following this sad event, Alan was kept busy with his work and Mo with sorting her mum's estate, of which she was the sole and meagre beneficiary; her mother had been as poor in material possessions as she had been rich in emotional and spiritual matters.

Mo had many sleepless nights, thinking, dreaming, worrying, grieving and every night questioning just what the letter would have said. Who was it to? Why didn't her mum start it? Why was she writing it and why was the little 'box of treasures' alongside? Were they connected?

Sleep came and went but the questions were always there, even in her dreams the questions came.

Mo even thought about visiting a medium or psychic or just about anybody that might be able to fill in the gaps. Mo kept putting it off though because Alan wasn't much of a believer in such strange goings on.

Then, one Thursday evening in September, on his return from work, Alan told her, 'Right Mo, that's it, get your bags packed and dig your walking boots out of the under stairs cupboard. We are off on a little holiday.'

'Oh, that's a lovely thought Al, it really is,' she replied warmly, 'but I don't think I'm up to it. . . and you have work tomorrow.'

'Nope! Got the day off - and Monday too. We're going and that's that. It will do you good to get away from this place and feel some fresh sea air, eat some good country food and maybe take a few walks on the moors too,' said Alan confidently as he held his head up high and smiled a smile of satisfaction.

'Moors?' Mo enquired, 'Where are we going then?'

'Never you mind, it's a mystery. No - it's a surprise. Everything is booked, all taken care of, already paid for, you'll like it, you'll see. So, sort out your gear and we're off at the crack of dawn. Okay perhaps not quite that early, and we'll buy a nice breakfast somewhere on the way.'

So it was to be, and on one fine early September Friday they arrived at Countisbury; it was about noon when Alan pulled into a large car park to the sound of city tyres on country stones.

'Here we are Mo, we've arrived - our new home for the next three nights,' announced an excited Alan. 'Let's grab our bags and register at the Inn then the afternoon is ours.' Mo was temporarily excited too, she had forgotten all her troubles; just for a while that is. Alan saw her mood change quickly as Mo noticed the old church and graveyard beyond the car park, her thoughts returning to her mum and the letter she never wrote. 'Come on, that's enough of that old girl, this is a lovely happy place, somewhere new that we've not seen before, it will be a lovely holiday. Let's see what they have for lunch - anything you want you can have.'

Mo snapped out of her thoughts, 'Of course, I'm sorry Al, I should be more thoughtful of you too. Let's treat ourselves; you can have a steak if you like.' So saying she threw her rucksack over one shoulder, picked up her handbag and they crossed briskly over the deserted roadway to the Inn.

It was a warm reception that welcomed them to their new 'home.' They settled into their upstairs room, situated above a quiet part of the building and with fine views of open countryside and a blue sky decorated with small white clouds. 'There, look at that,' said Alan. 'If God were to paint a picture then surely it would look like this. Come on, change of plan, let's have a light lunch and get out there amongst that lovely nature.'

'OK, love, I'll catch you up, I just want to lay here for a moment and enjoy the peace and quiet after the journey,' murmured Mo as she kicked her shoes off and reclined on the bed, her eyes almost closing as if to enjoy the peace all the more.

'Don't be too long,' replied Alan as he quietly closed the latched door behind him and softly descended the stairs to the bar area. The ground floor of the Inn was huge, very long with changes of levels and room widths; it looked to Alan as though it may have been extended or altered many times; it added to the charm, it added mystery. Alan soon made friends and chatted to a couple of pleasant local characters in the bar downstairs. Meanwhile, upstairs, as though someone who loved her had sent a gift, a gentle sleep overcame Mo. Almost as quickly she was visited by a strange dream. It was as though she had gone back in time and was sitting in a quiet corner of the Inn downstairs; the only light, the light of early morning, came in through some cobwebby windows to her right, wood smoke drifted from the open fire along an oak beamed ceiling and a smiling, plump faced, pretty girl in servants garb walked happily towards her from the far end of the long room; she was only a few feet away when the sound of a wagon and horses on the old earth and stone road outside reverberated through the Inn as though it really were there; It woke Mo with a start. Now wide awake she listened intently to an unexpected and all pervading silence then glanced at her watch; she hurriedly slipped on her shoes and went in search of Alan.

'Ah, there you are love, the landlady has made us some sandwiches and suggested a fine short walk to the headland where we can eat them and look across the sea to Wales. How's that?' said a beaming Alan.

Mo began, 'I've just had a strange dream. . .'

She was quickly interrupted by Alan, 'Come on Mo, we've had enough of dreams for a while, we're on holiday, let's enjoy our time here.' So saying he picked up the neatly wrapped sandwiches, took Mo by the arm, and led her out of the Inn door and into the bright world of a September Devon. Alan was going to do his utmost to help Mo out of the doldrums of the last six months; this was going to be a special holiday.

They walked through the churchyard and out to the headland. The landlady was right, it was a beautiful spot. They were blessed with warm sunshine, found a comfortable rock to sit on and were sheltered from a light breeze by a bank of gorse which still carried its alluring coconut scent. The sandwiches were excellent and time just seemed to disappear, being replaced by contentment. When the sunshine began to cool, their thoughts turned to the warm Inn and its open fire. 'Al, let's look around the church on the way back, I'd like that,' she said, standing and stretching her arms with pleasure.

'Okay,' Alan replied, adding, 'we'll have a night in by the fire, there's a nice one in a back room with settees by it. We can have a meal and a few drinks. We'll just chill out and enjoy our time . . . Right, the church it is. . .'

As they walked quietly alongside the outer wall of the churchyard towards the little wooden gate, Mo had a flashback to her earlier dream, a little shiver ran down her spine, she put it down to the cooling air and didn't mention it to Alan, he didn't seem to want to know these things. They spent a while reading the gravestones and wondering at the disparity of lifespan, there were those who made their eighties and some who never saw their first year out. 'Disease, probably,' intimated Alan, 'simple diseases we can treat now were killers then. How lucky we are to know all what we do these days.'

That evening they enjoyed a lovely meal, found one of the Inn's many quiet and secluded corners and played some of the board games the Inn had for guests. They played until Alan realised that perhaps he wasn't used to drinking so much and started losing the plot never mind the games. 'I'm off to bed love,' slurred Alan standing and knocking his legs against the low table they had been using.

'Okay dear, I'll be up shortly, I might see if I can get a hot chocolate,' Mo replied.

When Mo returned from the bar she was surprised to see another guest sitting there, a pleasant old lady with a motherly look to her. 'Oh, I'm sorry,' said Mo turning to go.

'You do no such thing my dear, you sit ee here. I be Grace Elworthy and I'm not about to turn you away.' Grace gestured reassuringly and smiled warmly.

Taking a seat opposite, Mo said considerately, 'I should leave you in peace really.'

'Ar, dear, we're all looking to find that,' Grace replied softly.

'I'm sure I've heard your name before?' quizzed Mo.

'Tis an old name round these parts, perhaps someone in the Inn mentioned it,' suggested Grace.

It was the beginning of a long and heartfelt conversation during which Mo told the lady all about her mum, the letter, Alan's work and how he was treating her to this special holiday.

'What a dear old soul,' thought Mo as she later climbed the stairs to bed. 'I feel so much better now.'

Later that night Mo had the dream again. She saw the same girl with the mop cap walking towards her from the far end of the long room, seeming to walk with real purpose but still smiling happily. Then something really strange happened: Mo *became* the girl in the dream; it was most odd, there were times when she felt that she was awake enough to tell herself this was a dream. The dream world and the waking world seemed in confusion. Mo, now as the servant girl, actually felt herself opening the Inn door, a different door to the one she knew as Mo the guest, stepping outside and down two steps onto an earth and stone roadway. It was early morning in the dream and to her right, in front of a small barn and a stable, was a young man preparing horses for a wagon. He had harness in hand but none the less lifted his cap and smiled coyly at her. Mo found herself responding: this young man was the love of her life. Up to then Mo hadn't noticed the iron pot she was carrying but now she did, for it slipped heavily from her hand and clattered loudly on the stones where it fell. The horses were spooked, became increasingly skittish and the young man struggled to calm them. He couldn't hold them both and one made off, bolting straight down the road and directly at Mo. Mo was frozen with fear, transfixed to the spot, the sound of hooves and the desperate cries of the young man filled her ears all in a distorted slow time. The last thing she heard was the horse's frenzied wild breath and the last thing she saw was the sky vanishing into blackness. Mo sat bolt upright in bed sweat pouring from her brow, her body fired with adrenalin, her breathing rapid and her hands trembling. Mo turned to Alan to wake him. . . tell him all about it. Mo stopped, looked at Alan snoring peacefully and determined to keep this silly dream to herself. Poor Alan had endured so much grief since her mum died he deserved this special holiday and he certainly didn't deserve being woken up at three in the morning by his crazy wife.

It was well over an hour before Mo slept again, there were no more such dreams. Still, she was up early in the morning and with questions to ask. She pulled the duvet around her Alan's sleeping shoulders and quietly crept downstairs in search of breakfast, and some answers too.

Mo was too early for breakfast so she found a quiet corner in which to think on the nightmare of last night. She was so lost in thought Mo didn't notice her new found friend and confidante, the little old lady Grace, join her at the table. 'Good morning, dear,' said Grace quietly.

'Oh, hello Grace, not sure it's all that good mind you. I had a nightmare last night. . . saw a young lady die in an accident with a horse - right outside that door it was.' Mo shuddered.

'Don't you worry about things like that dear, all such things can be explained. I've not been about all these years without taking an interest in such matters,' Grace paused for a moment, and then continued, 'I'll tell you all about it later. I think I hear your husband coming and you should enjoy each other's company without some old lady hanging around. Look for me when you have some quiet time and I'll tell you all.' Grace stood quietly with ease and left. Mo was just thinking how well Grace walked for an old lady of her age when Alan arrived.

'Morning Mo, crikey, what a night that was! I shan't be drinking as much today. How did you sleep? Come on, I think breakfast is ready through the back room.' Alan pointed animatedly in the direction of breakfast and gestured with the other hand for Mo to join him.

Alan and Mo sat opposite each other at the pine table and breakfast was brought in by the landlord himself, who placed the plates gently, asking if there was anything else.

'No, we're fine, thanks,' said Alan. The landlord turned to leave. 'No, wait a minute please,' said Mo, holding her knife and fork at the ready. Can I ask you a question?' The landlord nodded thoughtfully and Mo continued, 'Tell me, do you have ghosts here? Do you know anything about a young woman, probably a servant, who was killed by a horse outside your very door?'

The landlord smiled and said, 'Ghosts? I can't say as I've seen any and we've been here a few years now. Sometimes the locals speak of such things but I think the spirits are mainly in the bottles or in the customers. Mind you, occasionally I'll hear the odd noise - but that's to be expected with an old creaky building like this one - even the wind howls by the door frame when it blows from the north.' He paused and thoughtfully put his hand under his chin, before continuing, 'I've done lots of research on the building and its occupants and never come across any death of a young woman. Anyway, I mustn't keep you; your breakfast will get cold.' He bowed his head slightly, turned and left for the kitchen.

Alan hadn't been listening that intently but asked, 'Wow, what was that all about then?' Mo didn't want to disturb Alan about her dream; he needed this holiday probably more than she.

'Oh, nothing really love, I just get the feeling that we are not alone here sometimes.'

'You're right, we're not,' said Alan sternly, we're being watched as we speak. This was most unusual for Alan to take such things so seriously and it surprised Mo, even startled her a little. Alan continued, 'See, over there? I see eyes; watching us from by the doorway?' Mo hardly dared to turn her head to look. 'I reckon he's after one of these sausages!' Alan laughed and was back to his normal self as Mo turned to see the big black dog who lived at the Inn staring intently not at her but at the table and its contents.

She had to laugh herself, she needed to lighten up, she'd made something out of nothing. . . time to forget it and finish breakfast. 'What shall we do today then Al,' Mo smiled, 'take that dog for a walk?' They both laughed; it was a special holiday after all.

'There's a lovely old lady called Grace who's staying here, you must meet her sometime, she's a real angel, great to chat to about life,' confided Mo.

'Yes, there are some wonderful people around here. I was talking with a couple of locals at the bar and they told me that there's a spectacular geological fault called the Valley of the Rocks. They told me how to get there and that it was worth the effort, but that the Inn is renowned for its excellent Sunday lunches and we mustn't miss it - people come twenty miles just for the dinner. I do just love a Sunday roast,' said Alan looking wistfully into the future. . . almost certainly at a Sunday lunch.

'Okay, Valley of the Rocks, here we come. We'll walk off the breakfast before you restock with lunch. I sometimes wonder if anything else but food occupies your mind. Come on, teeth cleaned and boots on, let's be having you,' she chuckled to herself, threw her paper napkin remonstratively onto her empty plate and went to prepare herself for the next adventure.

The couple enjoyed a bracing walk in the Valley of the Rocks, it was a little colder than they expected as much of the path didn't see the Sun until afternoon. None the less it was exhilarating and they took a few photos of Castle Rock and the odd wild goat or two to take home for the album. They were pleased to return to the warmth of the Inn and even more pleased with the roast dinner. As the Sunday lunchtime diners started to thin out and go home, Alan and Mo enjoyed a few drinks and chatted with a local farmer and his wife. God, life was good on holiday, if not quite so good for farming; hedge cutting, ploughing and storing the winter feed, all needed doing. Alan enjoyed hearing of the practicalities of life on the moors, and enjoyed the fact they weren't his to worry about. God, life was good on holiday. As the last of the customers left the Inn for home, the tables were cleared and wiped by staff before they too disappeared into the kitchen. Suddenly all was quiet and Alan was struck by a bout of tiredness. 'Must have been all that talk of work on the farm,' he told Mo.

'More like that big dinner and the few drinks that followed,' laughed Mo, 'why don't you go and lie down for a bit, I'll stay down here and read a while - I've seen a nice book of short stories about somewhere; it has a nice red cover with a table, a candle and a letter, looks interesting. Off you go, I'm fine.'

Good as the book might be it was not why Mo wanted to stay in the bar, she hoped that Grace might still be at the Inn; Mo had noticed that Grace wasn't one for crowds; in fact she'd noticed that Grace even avoided Alan, despite Mo desperately wanting him to meet her. As Mo searched and rounded one of the quiet corners of the long room she almost bumped into Grace coming the other way, 'Oh, hello,' they both said in unison just like twins.

'Well, my dear, now there's no one about to listen to our conversation so I reckons I can tell you what you wanted to know. Let's sit by the inglenook, it be warmer there for ee. No one will come back in the bar until later this afternoon. They have their own dinners now and forty winks after,' said Grace with a wink of her own. 'About your dreams; they were more than dreams - sometimes they are you know. I sense I can tell you these things as it's your time to know. You saw the girl, well, young woman really, because you were seeking something beyond your own living world. Your mind was open and receptive, that's how she could share with you her own experiences. It happened long ago, she was an orphan, only known by the name of Hannah. In fact she was about twenty three or four when she was killed, not so long before she was due to marry. I reckon that would be about 1892.

As you said, she was a chubby faced, happy girl with a great purpose in life; she never fulfilled it and her spirit stays here trying to complete that something that can never be.

The stable lad never stopped loving her and he never married another. He's buried over in the churchyard across the road, though not near Hannah; she was a pauper you see and buried in common ground with no marker. He has a grave marker, even if it is much worn and hard to find now, but his spirit was content with what he had done in life, his sacrifice and dedication to Hannah, so his spirit has moved on. I sense your mum has moved on too, she was content with life, she could see you were happy and that was her one true purpose in life, just to see her daughter happy. I think this holiday was as much her idea as it was Alan's. He was suddenly inspired to act; a seed was planted in his mind and his heart answered. I also think that seeing Hannah is also a message just for you. Many might feel her presence but precious few will ever see her as you have done. It's a message that tells you there is somewhere else to go beyond death. Those who have fulfilled their purpose in life simply move on and those that have yet to do so struggle to find a way onward. In consequence they can relive their demise over and over, trying to find a way of atonement, trying to find redemption, a way out of the spiritual prison their own mind created. I also think that Hannah had a message for you too - about being happy. Hannah didn't question about her parents' life or death, she lived her orphan life as best she could, as happy as she could. For all her problems she was a happy girl. There's the answer you seek: be happy. It is what your mother would have written had she the time. Your mum sent you this message, this special holiday and today of all days you can be happy again. I've said too much I'm sure, I must leave you now to think, and smile. I must go; I have other things to attend to now. Perhaps I'll see you before you leave.'

Mo so wanted to hug that dear little old motherly lady that had befriended her so kindly but it didn't seem appropriate at the time. She'd see her later. Mo was at peace, the peace she had sought for months. With a smile on her face and a skip in her step she went in search of Alan, to wake him and take him out for a walk to clear the cobwebs; or perhaps just quietly lay down beside him and sleep a happy dreamless sleep.

**

Come Monday afternoon the car was running well, almost as though it knew it was on the way home and the Autumn Sun shone brightly all around. The road was quiet, the car was quiet and Alan drove slowly so as to enjoy the experience, he felt good, all was well with the world, a beautiful world. Deep wooded combes gave way to undulating hills and views of the Somerset levels; he took the view in like taking a long and welcome breath.

'That was a great little holiday, wasn't it Mo?' said Alan rhetorically. 'And we didn't think once about your mum's letter either; I wonder what she would have written.'

Mo reached out and touched his hand, 'sometimes there are no answers; sometimes you don't need the questions either; we might never know but our soul will.' She smiled a contented smile and looked out of the window to enjoy the rest of her journey; as she did so, her mind wandered back to the last few minutes at the Inn. Alan was carrying their bags out to the car when Mo looked for Grace one more time, she was not to be found in all her usual haunts but Mo did find the landlord checking the bar stock. 'Thank you so much for a wonderful holiday,' she said. 'Can you tell me where I can find Grace, she helped me so much and I want to say thank you and goodbye.'

'Grace?' enquired the landlord, always willing to help if he could.

'Yes, Grace Elworthy, the lovely old lady that's been staying here for the last few days.'

The landlord put down the dust cloth and bottle, slowly turned with a puzzled look on his face to look Mo in the eyes and said, 'But Maureen, you and Alan have been our only guests this weekend. No one else is staying here.'

'No argument is so convincing as is the evidence of your own eyes.'

AN ANNIVERSARY GIFT FROM EXMOOR.
(An Exmoor ghost story.)

Jingling a set of anxious car keys in his pocket, the Estate Agent leaned on the hallway newel post, looked up the wide, carpet-less Edwardian staircase and called out, 'Yes, lady, the attic does need to be emptied; if you like I can call in a house clearance chap we know and just add it to the bill for you.'

'It's okay,' replied Gillian. 'I'll do it myself, after all he was my Uncle - I owe him that at least.'

The Agent's goodbyes were lost to her ears as Gillian flicked on the switch to a dust-covered electric light bulb in the attic. Amid the strange, distinctive smell of hot dust and old papers Gillian began to examine her lately deceased uncle's 'treasures.'

For many years her uncle had been a rural journalist in the South West. His quiet non-intrusive nature had earned him much respect and trust, a trust he had never betrayed; his friendly nature had endeared him to the public through whom he sought an honest living. A good and honourable man; now he was passed to the other side and Gillian was determined to handle his estate with justly due respect.

It wasn't long before Gillian became aware of some old diaries and notes from the nineteen sixties; there was something about them that made her want to pick them up and hold them close; it was almost as though she was meant to find them.

Turning off the attic light as she left, Gillian retired to a comfortable sunlit room at the back of the house; it was a room that overlooked a wild but pleasant garden, a garden that seemed to be looking in on her as much as she looked out on it. Gillian sat in a high-backed armchair by the window and placed the papers on her lap. Smiling to herself, she thought, 'I bet this was Uncle's favourite chair,' and then she began to read.

This is what she found:

Note for file.
Interview with Edward and Alexandra Hilyard, Monday 19th September 1964. Reference a strange and ghostly experience on the moor.

Edward Hilyard seemed a man ever angry with the world yet never so with his dear wife of some forty good years. Alexandra Hilyard was born about the same time as her husband during Queen Victoria's last days in 1901. Alexandra was not a well lady, a victim to a terminal illness she decidedly wished to keep to herself, she suspected this would be her last year. . . she had not told her husband in order to save him from the premature burden of knowing. Edward remained oblivious to the facts; she said it was better this way. This was the weekend of their fortieth wedding anniversary and their trip from the midlands in their old Morris Minor to Exmoor was a special gift to each other in celebration.

As Gillian leafed through the pages of notes, a scrap of paper fluttered floorwards, she caught it easily in her hand; in a red inked scrawl of forceful and jagged handwriting it read:

Utter rubbish! This newspaper is not a comic - do not submit any more rubbish of this sort again.

It was signed by her uncle's editor of the day, the pressure of his pen had almost broken through the paper. 'Obviously not a believer,' decided Gillian as she resumed the fascinating study of her uncle's notes. 'Poor old Uncle.'

<u>Alexandra Hilyard's statement</u>:-

'We were so tired from our long journey but were still excited
about staying for the weekend at our hotel on Exmoor. It was
late afternoon and a grey mist had descended on some sign-
less and narrow moorland road we had taken. I never was
any good with maps, ours didn't show those little roads anyway and we never once came across anyone to ask. We
seemed to crawl along blindly for an eternity, the fog was
thicker now and soon it was dark too, about half past six or
so I think, poor Edward could hardly see the way forward,
the lights on our little car aren't that good you know, he kept
to the road by following the verge on the left, it's all we could
do, that and hope we'd come to a village soon. . . but we
didn't. He said he was worried about the petrol running out.
It was getting colder and the car heater never was much good
at the best of times. I started to pray for a miracle and then
one happened: two great stone built gate posts appeared just
off the road to the left.

The gravel drive looked good and Edward said it must go to
a big house or a farm. He said we should go down there and
'throw ourselves upon their mercy as strangers hopelessly
lost on the moor,' he said.
From what little we could see through the fog it was a grand
double fronted mansion with a central great door, it was so
quaint and rustic with the soft light of oil lamps either side.
It looked big enough to be a hotel, we decided to ask if we
could stay or at least have directions to help us on our way.
We approached the doorway more frightened of the fog on
the moors than we were of knocking a stranger's door at
night. They had one of those old fashioned bell pull rods that
rang a bell by cable, you must know the sort I mean, but they
are usually so old they don't work anymore. It wasn't long
before the door opened to a very polite young lady with im-
peccable manners, dressed in maid's clothing; all in a heavy
dark dress to the ground with a white apron and mop cap -
pretty as a picture. She made a tiny gesture like a curtsy and
invited us in as though we were expected. 'Come on you
through to the drawing room sir, we have a warm fire waiting
for you,' she'd said in a soft Devon accent. Well Edward liked

that, I can tell you, not only welcomed in but a warm fire and being called 'sir,' that was a first for him I can tell you. She took our coats and insisted we stayed the night, 'people suffer miserably and even die out there on the moors in fog like this,' she'd said, 'you're welcome to stay the night. We so rarely see visitors these days. I'll just ask you to be sure to leave early before the young master returns home in the morning. Best to go before he comes home at daybreak as he's been a touch angry these days. Don't you be telling anyone I said that mind you. I'll fetch you a bite to eat and have your bed warmed for you.'

We couldn't believe our luck, what a dear young thing to help us so and what an amazing house it was too. The drawing room was full of grand furniture, large gilt framed paintings adorned the walls, candles burned in Georgian brass candle-sticks and a decorative oil lamp, like my grandmother used before she had electricity, reflected light off the highly pol-ished surface of a circular mahogany table. I remember Ed-ward saying that they probably couldn't get the electric so far out on the moor and that it was a good job they didn't have a lot of visitors as, sure as eggs is eggs, all those fine antiques the place was full of would soon be knocked off by burglars if they knew about them.
We sat by the great carved marble fire place with our feet out towards that lovely fire. . . oh, how that fire seemed to solve all our problems at a stroke.

Our dear young hostess soon brought us both some warm milk, wonderful cheese and pieces of the finest home cooked ham I've ever seen or tasted. As I turned to thank her I caught a glimpse of what I can only guess were deer hounds or something similar; great big rough coated dogs, a pair of them, padded silently by the open doorway along the flag stones of the hall outside and towards the main door. Edward was too slow to look up from his plate and see them but he assured me they would be friendly, 'throw them a bit of ham if you're worried,' he joked with me. I'd not seen Edward so happy with the world for many a year. It brought a smile to my face, yet a tear to my heart, what with me knowing all what I do and all that. Later that night as we lay in bed, a nice cosy bed it was too, how they warmed it up without electric I have no idea, anyway, as we lay in bed, a night candle burning warmly by our side, we talked of our day and the adventure we had endured and now so enjoyed. Edward said that it couldn't have been a better anniversary gift if we'd planned it this way, it was the very stuff of life itself, he'd said. I began to wonder if the place was in fact a hotel of sorts as I'd seen other guests on the upstairs landing going quietly to their rooms, some dressed in the fashions of bygone years. I hadn't spoken to them as they seemed to be quite lost in their own thoughts and with everywhere as quiet as the grave I didn't want to spoil their stay. I thought perhaps we'd all meet up and chat at breakfast but as it happened we didn't see them again, for we left just about dawn as requested by the kindly young maid. She was such a little sweetie that we couldn't let her down and get her in any trouble with the master of the house. We'd slept warm and safe until it was time to leave in our little car; we thanked God we hadn't remained lost out on the moor. There was a little mist still but the maid said it would soon clear and we would find our way towards town if we turned right at the end of the drive and stayed on the main thoroughfare; she stood on the steps and waved us goodbye with a cheery, 'God speed and safe journey.'

Edward was concentrating on his driving, as he always did, but I observed a frenzied rider approaching the house across the fields, he was riding hard, whipping his lathered horse and with a thunder-black look upon his face. No wonder that poor soul wanted us away before his return I thought. As we passed through the stone gateposts they looked quite different from the night before, they now looked unkempt and almost derelict, had they looked like that when we arrived I doubt Edward would have ventured along that overgrown driveway. I'm not sure if I heard screaming and shouting behind us but what with Edward changing gear and humming some happy song to himself I can't for sure ever say that I did now. On coming to a small hamlet we checked our directions with a couple of hedge layers walking their way to work.

When we told them of our lucky overnight stay they were be-mused and told us there was no such place. They insisted that, knowing the moors as they did, they knew more than us and we must be mistaken! We decided to stay one last night in the hotel in town and the landlord put us on to you to hear of our strange tale.... and there, now you have heard it.'

Interview concluded 11.30 am. 19th September 1964

**

'**Additional Historical Research - note for file**: the remote Wyke Grange, built some thirty years previous (about 1860) by a family of Lancashire mill owners, burned to the ground with a total loss of life on Friday 18th September 1891. The young owner, a Mr Edward Lightfoot Esquire tragically per-ished in the flames and this only one day before he was due to marry a local young woman of independent means. The cause of the fire remains unknown but preparations for a grand weekend celebration are thought to have contributed to the blaze. The fire would have burned unnoticed and un-controlled for some considerable time and the building was so severely damaged that no bodies or remains thereof could be found for decent Christian burial. (They lay there still and will forever more.) Edward Lightfoot's bride to be refused to discuss the matter when questioned and it was said by a close friend that she had in fact already previously planned to leave the County; she asked for privacy in her grief.'

**

Gillian tried to share her exciting find with many but when confronted by continuing disbelief she eventually threw the papers away, never to speak openly of them again. Doubting listeners had always glibly 'explained away' the story with their own superior views; yet none dissuaded her from the trust in her uncle's judgement, he was an honest man. . . she owed him that at least.

Author's note:

Today, any and all remains of the Wyke Grange, including the gate posts and drive, are lost to the moor and gorse. There are precious few records of its short existence. Young Master Lightfoot, a commonly angry man with all the world, suddenly jilted by his bride to be, destroyed and burned all about him in a crazed fit of rejection and madness.

The 'guests' that Alexandra saw at the Grange that night perhaps were other lost travellers lured in by the gate posts and lamps of the Grange as they sought sanctuary from the moorland fog but for some unknown reason they had not left the house before the master returned; so condemned to remain forever in a place that does not exist in real time.

If you venture to ask, you'll find those who work the moors nearby will shake their heads and deny they have ever seen the old stone gate posts half hiding in the mist. They prefer not to know, not to tell, a wisdom perhaps you might consider yourself.

**

'The way you wake up is the way you live your life.'

ONLY WORDS

Fleeting summer joys now only treasured memory, a biting November wind picked up from the East. Seemingly it blew right through him, sending its icy touch beyond his tattered winter great coat to grip his bones beneath, though his heart, as yet unchanged, remained both warm and steadfast.

The undeniable curtain of dusk was fast drawing closed.

At such a time when the darkling arrives and dims nature's light for sleep, he stood in silence, alone yes but perhaps not lonely at the far end of the old pier.

The pier was an enduring legacy from the once powerful empire days of Victoria. Despite abundant signs of dereliction and self sacrifice to the elements, the pier still stood courageous and noble, a warrior leaning out into the wilding and all embracing sea.

It was his ritual to stand there every evening at the end of the pier. He had never missed a day, not one day had he missed, yet few if any would ever notice him.

He would stand and look out to sea while dreaming of the love he had been denied in life. He was but a poor man and she, the dutiful daughter of an intensely rich and scheming merchant.

His own impoverished hovel he shared with reluctant rats that weren't that keen on such enforced frugality or the resident cold and damp either; her home was warm, lavish, grand

and spacious, rich with tapestry curtains, sparkling with engraved glass and glittering with servant polished silver.

He had come to realise, if he truly loved her enough, that there could be no other way to keep her always in his heart. To be sure, it would please her father.

He turned up his coat collar, sensitively fastening the top button that clung uncertainly to its place in life by a couple of worn threads. With the ease and strength of youth, he climbed effortlessly and silently up onto the broad railings.

He stood only briefly before he fell. He fell to meet the freedom promised him by the ocean.

In the hundred and twenty three years that have since elapsed, he never missed a day. Each and every evening at dusk he returns to the pier and each and every evening he stands, he climbs and he falls to seek the freedom that eludes him still.

Perhaps you've seen him.

**

'The feelings we feel are created by the thoughts we think.'

Supernatural Tales

THE WELCOMED STRANGER

The tale of a young man's strange
and supernatural adventure
near Countisbury, where
moor meets sea.

Sam was a tall, strong young man in his early twenties;
staunch defender of a fiercely independent and self-
reliant nature, a trait he'd no doubt inherited from his
Celtic ancestors.

Despite all his youth, strength and adventuring experience,
as he approached from the Churchyard track, he was very
happy to see signs of life and the early morning smoke rising
from the chimney of the Blue Ball Inn, very happy indeed.

Though he was all night tired and hungry, he had a compelling tale to tell and tell it he must.

The landlord, an affable gentleman with a welcoming smile,
observed him through the small casement windows as Sam
crossed the road with determined gait and lengthening strides
towards the Inn. The landlord slid the bolts and opened
the heavy oak Inn door, a large long-haired black dog stood
curious at his side.

'I'm sorry sir, we don't open until later. . .' the landlord's
voice trailed off as an inner voice told him something strange
was afoot. His dog backed away silently and deeper into the
old Inn. 'Never you mind the time though sir, you come on
in, come on in and sit yourself by the fire; we have some soup
warming.'

Sam interrupted him, 'Can it wait a while? I must tell someone what happened to me last night; someone must believe me. Well to be honest I'm not certain what really happened at all, perhaps it was all a dream. . . but then, how did I get here?'

'Here, sit you down there sir,' reiterated the landlord, pointing to an upright wooden chair opposite an inglenook fireplace, the source of the smoke that had first welcomed Sam to Countisbury. The landlord carefully placed a fresh dry log and poked the fire thoughtfully. He asked, 'So what's your name sir, and what brings you to our door this winter's morning?'

'I'm Sam, Samuel Richmond, I should have been here last night. I've bed and breakfast booked.' Sam forced a smile and a pretend laugh. 'Too late for the bed I suppose, though I'd love a breakfast - but only when I've told you what happened first.'

The landlord nodded, held his hand up as if to say, 'One moment,' then called towards the kitchen and his wife, 'Guest for breakfast dear; make it a big one.' His wife poked her head through the open doorway by the bar, smiled, nodded in acknowledgement and disappeared again. 'You'll not be disappointed Mr Richmond,' the landlord assured him. 'So how is it you didn't arrive last night then?'

'Yesterday I was visiting friends over at Yenworthy Cottage, they're writers you know, well Robert is and his wife Beth is an archaeologist with a big university somewhere up north. They'd rented the cottage for six months, she's researching some old myths and legends about Viking raids along the Devonian coast and Robert is writing a book on the same sort of thing; he's calling it Dragon's Lair or was it Wolf's Lair. . . can't remember exactly, it's all made up stuff that he writes - interesting none the less. I'd had a great day with them, a really interesting couple, passionate about their work, particularly Beth who couldn't wait to show me some old human bones she had recently unearthed. She obviously didn't consider it disturbing the peace of the dead; it was just science to her. I stayed for a relaxed and pleasant lunch then we had a short walk to look at the sea. I was leaving it a bit late to get here by that time and they told me I should stay overnight with them and walk here the next day in good light. But I didn't listen, I don't like to let people down and it's not more than a few miles along the coastal tracks. I collected my small overnight bag, nothing special in it and certainly nothing to equip me for the night that was to confront me and my sanity. Then I said my goodbyes to them, nearly for good too as it happened. I can't say I wasn't warned you know, they both said more than once I should be watchful for the sea mist coming in before dark and how dangerous it was along the combe edges. I told 'em straight, 'Don't you be worrying about me, I'll be fine, and such a stroll in the park won't be a problem for me.' Well, I set off at a goodly pace along the wooded track towards the sea, all was going well, a few ups and downs as you know but going okay; the track was fairly clear to follow and I couldn't see it being a problem to arrive here either before or just after dusk.

I'd walked about an hour or more when it happened; in the blink of an eye the mist fell on me from all sides, as if it had been waiting in hiding for me, I couldn't see much at all, I lost sight of the track, in fact it was almost as though it vanished in front of my eyes, as if it wasn't there in the first place. I was committed by then, it was as bad or maybe worse to try and go back to Yenworthy. I have to confess I was filled with much regret and I'm not ashamed to say, a little fear, for the darkening night was cold and the mist was already eating into my bones. I knew well enough to keep away from the cliff edges and that I had perhaps three steep valleys to cross before I'd be out of the trees or come across the road. I was filled with such a sense of loss that it was as though nothing I knew existed anymore; my only proof of existence was a few feet of un-trod ground around me; No torch had I nor could I read my watch; I listened hard for the sound of the sea or of streams running seaward but the mist smothered all sound, I could hardly hear my own footfalls. I spoke loudly to myself, 'Sam you idiot,' I said, 'you have done for yourself, now damn well get yourself out of this mess, come on get me out of here.' God alone knows who I was talking to but talk I did. I knew I couldn't stay on the ridges but would have to drop down into a valley and up the other side. I thought that if trees could grow on the slopes then I could climb them too, it didn't work out like that. I made many small detours searching for invisible footholds with my blind feet while my cold hands grasped equally blindly for twigs or branches to keep my balance.

I was tiring quickly and the damp was truly biting bone deep, I began to feel the cold of the already dead. I'd always said I didn't need the help or advice of others, that I could do it all on my own but now a new truth was thrust upon me.

Half way up a steep and thicket strewn incline, my feet slipping on muddy slopes and thorns tearing at my clothes as if to hold me there, my legs began to fail and I thought to myself that this was the end of me; if they ever looked for or found my body they couldn't know the horrors that I felt last night. Then, as if by some magic, my feet found themselves on flat ground and I stood on a narrow ledge, my legs shaking with exertion and adrenalin and me thinking I was losing my mind, hallucinating perhaps. But it was no illusion - there in front of me was a small stone and timber hut and better still, it was showing a light. With a fresh lease of life in body and in spirit I made my way to the hut and peered in through the wooden bars of a small glassless window; there was nobody in but a fire was burning in a simple earth hearth. I tried the door, it was primitive but opened well enough; I went in and sat on a bench like log near the fire and warmed my hands. . . oh, heaven it was to feel the mist dry out from my clothes and bones. I was sure that whoever lived there would return soon and I mentally prepared a little speech of thanks, apologies and the like that befits having entered someone's home uninvited. Though time seemed almost alien in that place, I glanced at my watch in the firelight; I cursed, it seemed to have stopped and it was a treasured gift from my long lost father. I put another log on the fire; there was a small stack near the bench within easy reach and a larger stack over by the far wall to my left. I sat in relative peace and calm with my speech in mind. Then the door opened and all my plans went out the window as I observed the owner of the hut standing in the doorway. He was shorter than us but stocky with one or two big scars on his bearded face, his hair nearly obscured his piercing eyes with a fringe that looked slightly reddish in the fire light, his clothes were simple and looked like he'd made them for himself from whatever he could find or kill in the woods. He wore a stout leather belt which held an ancient looking axe at his side, his hand was on the axe shaft and his thumb caressed the curved blade. My speech had gone, not just what to say but the ability to say it too, I was gripped with fear. He came into the hut and closed the door, all the while looking in my direction and then he sat opposite me on a similar log bench like the one which I had taken. Still thumbing the axe blade, he stared, almost as though he knew something that I did not, straight into my eyes. The only sound was my own breath and heartbeat. The fire began to die down and the room become darker, he gestured to me with his head and eyes to put another log on the fire, which I did so very carefully. God, I was tired, I have no idea what time it was or how long I'd been in the hut. I dared not sleep, I had to stay awake. The fire died down yet again and soon all the spare wood was used, I scraped together a few bits of bark and twigs and threw them on the fire which seemed as pleased as I to see the dancing flames warm the room, but soon they too were gone. As the hut cooled I went to stand and fetch a log from the other stack by the wall, as I did so, that stocky little man reacted sharply and gripped the axe handle as though to tell me to stay where I was. . . or else . . . or else I might die? Only God knows the answer.

'Now and then the fatigue of exhaustion sought to close my unwilling eyes. Restless fears wrenched them open with a start - the dreadful apparition still before me, his own ever wakeful eyes staring straight into mine. Try as I might I could not keep my eyes open and must have slipped into a deep and desperate sleep, and now, this is the strangest of all things, when I finally awoke to a chilly but mist free dawn, the strange man had gone, so had the fire, the logs and the hut, all gone.

I stood on the flat ledge and looked around in bewilderment. There, where the second log stack had been and which my intimidating and forbidding host had stopped me from reaching, there was nothing but space, a sheer drop to rocks and a stream far below. I would have doubtlessly fallen to my death had I stepped there in the night for firewood, my broken body would have been meat for the rat, the fox and the raven.

Once the light of day had frightened the mist into the shadows I could so easily see my way forward and it wasn't so long before the path became clear all the way to the Inn. I left behind me on that flat ledge, thin grass mounds that still tell the world where walls once stood and perhaps, who knows, it was not so very long ago. I also left behind me eternal gratitude for a life saved; my own.'

The landlord's wife called through that breakfast was ready and was to be had in the kitchen. As Sam tucked into a hearty fried breakfast, the landlord suggested, 'Your room is booked till midday, why not have a rest and stay for a pub lunch before moving on.' The welcomed stranger was a welcomed guest once more. Sam nodded in agreement and glanced at his watch. . . he looked up and smiled. . . it was working again.

**

Author's note: I've revisited the Inn many a time and never heard the landlord speak again of that night, nor did Sam ever tell his tale to any other living soul. Sam left the Inn shortly after lunch and long before dark. He was not to be heard of again in these parts. Only you and whoever inhabits the unearthly world of the sea mist know the truth. If I may be so bold, I suggest, if you know what's good for you, you will neither tell what you know, nor venture out when the sea mist threatens the night. Better you stay in and read a book by the inglenook - you don't have to heed my advice.

**

'Experience is one thing you can't get for nothing'

Oscar Wilde

FATE AND THE NIGHT OF THE CARDS

Rowena, cup and plate in hand, walked from her modest living room to wash her tea time dishes in the kitchen; a puzzling noise stopped her dead in her tracks. She stood motionless and hushed, listening intently; she wasn't sure, but then, there it was again; it was a gentle, almost reticent knocking at her front door.

She walked questioningly along the boarded hallway to the front door of her humble terraced house. The door opened directly onto the pavement outside where the evening mist had conspired with the dim street lights to colour the deserted street a shadowy urban grey.

She tidied her shawl around her shoulders then pulled open the door cautiously. Before it was fully open, a man's voice inquired, 'Mrs Henderson? Mrs Rowena Henderson?'

There seemed no menace in the man's voice and she answered, 'Yes, that's me. What can I do for you?'

'I saw your compelling advert in the post office window, the one advertising card readings, I'm afraid I talked the shop keeper into telling me where you lived, sorry. I know it is an imposition; you can say no, if you like, but please don't. I really need a card reading; it must be tonight, there may never be another chance.'

His voice sounded more desperate and hopeful than dangerous to Rowena, so she stood to one side of the doorway and said, 'Well dear, you'd better come through then, it's getting damp out there and we can't read cards on the doorstep can we?' Rowena closed the door behind him and ushered him along the short hallway to the one presentable room she used for general living and eating.

'Pop your coat on the back of that chair and sit yourself at the table,' said Rowena clearing a space and reaching for a pack of cards from one of the table's two drawers. 'What shall I call you? And what exactly is it you want to find out?' She asked with a smile.

For some reason the questions noticeably surprised him, as if he wasn't expecting any questions coming his way. . . 'Er, Just call me, er, call me John. . . and what ever you tell me will be what I want; I'll leave it all in your hands. Thank you.'

'Okay John, just hold this pack of cards for me, use both hands, we don't want to miss anything do we? I'll be back in a moment; I'll just put the kettle on.'

Rowena filled and started the kettle going, this public card reading was a new and enforced venture for her; she was short of money since she and her husband had parted company. He was an addicted gambler, not a bad man other than that, but the gambling was all to live and die for. The distress had been too much for her to endure so she'd rented this little terrace and had begun a new life. Rowena worked in a local care home and, as she had been adept from childhood at reading cards, thought she might supplement her meagre income with a few readings. The kettle boiled and she went to the doorway to ask if John would like a cup of tea. Once again he appeared nervous and seemed to have taken an openly intrusive interest in the contents of the room, particularly Rowena's family photos, 'Oh, tea please, two sugars, er thank you, Mrs Henderson,' he replied.

Rowena was beginning to become uneasy herself now, 'Steady on old girl,' she calmed herself silently, 'stay composed and don't let on; everything will be fine, come on take the tea in, light a candle and put the bright light out then he can't be nosing around the room with his prying eyes. I wonder who he really is; perhaps the cards will tell.'

The cups chinked in the saucers and the bright light was replaced by a warming beeswax candle flame. 'Do you live alone then, Mrs Henderson?' asked John as though he already knew the answer.

'Yes, and I have done for nearly a year now,' Rowena replied, at once regretting not saying that she didn't and her burly ex-army husband would be arriving home at any minute. But it wasn't her way; she was inherently kindly and honest. 'Come on now John, if you want this card reading you must concentrate; relax but concentrate on the matter in hand. I want you to shuffle the pack, any way you like, just shuffle the cards and think on your questions.'

'Right John, keeping the cards face down I'd like you now to pick ten cards from the pack, it doesn't matter how you do it; if you wish you can spread them all over the table. It will almost feel like the card chooses you. You will just know the right ones. Take your time.'

Rowena watched as the stranger's strong and rough hands hovered over various cards then struggled to pick them up with his short fingernails, but she didn't intervene and he seemed to have considerable patience. Eventually John picked ten cards and held them up triumphantly with a glimmer of wonderment in his eyes. 'There, they all picked me, just like you said they would Mrs Henderson; Amazing; I've never had a card reading before, that was amazing, I just knew which ones to avoid and which to pick. I can already see this is going to be well worth my while.'

'Okay John, now I want you to make sure that the cards are in the right order, you need to use the same feeling you had when you picked them; shuffle or move them about until something tells you their place is right,' Rowena said quietly as she finished her now lukewarm tea. She leant back in her chair, observed his mannerisms and his obvious lack of card handling skills, it made her wonder why a card reading was so important to a man who couldn't even make a decent stab at shuffling the deck properly.

'All done Mrs Henderson, they feel just right now, should I turn them over?'

Rowena put out a hand to stop him, 'No John, I need to lay them out in a special way called the Celtic cross first, then if you still want you can turn them over one at a time. That may seem unusual in card reading circles; however, I can't see that, who does what, will change the outcome.'

**

The reading progressed apace; each new card only had the simplest of messages for Rowena to share with John. She had explained that she would be honest about what she saw in the cards but that often the best interpretation of what she saw would be in John's own heart and mind.

After a while she asked, 'So John, is it making sense to you so far? We have touched on an early love or emotion that relates to an older fair haired woman. That love was intuitive, the card of the Moon, the mother, but was held back or obstructed by a new emotional beginning, a new love. As far as learning goes you are doing well, nearly there, and your learning is strongly positive in direction,' she nodded to him to turn the next card.

For some reason John struggled to turn over this next card, almost as though he didn't want to know anymore or it didn't want to know him, but slowly, the eight of spades came into view and he pressed it down firmly on the table with his fingers.

John sensed Rowena's silence, 'is this a bad card Mrs Henderson?'

Rowena's mind was racing, 'No, not exactly bad John. . . I mean it could be or it might not be.' As Rowena looked across the table into John's face she could see the spectres of doubt and fear beginning to take hold of him as if they'd physically entered the room to take him away, 'Okay John, it's not necessarily bad, it is the card of fate, it's the card of Saturn, and it also foretells of struggle or conflict; I can see these very things so clearly in you now, so this card and what it means, is most important for you.'

Rowena wasn't normally inclined to try and guide the client's thinking but she was going to make an exception in John's case, it looked like it was sorely needed. 'Right John, if indeed that is your real name, fate is not always bad, we just tend to think it is, but some might say the winner of the lottery, I wish, was fated to win for some reason or another. It might have been fate that led you to the post office and to my little advert. . . was it fate that persuaded the nice people in the post office to give you my address? See, fate is not always the demon we make it out to be. Also consider the word struggle; notice, John, in the cards there is no portent about losing; it merely tells us that you face a struggle. Whether you win or not is going to be up to you, the cards cannot give you any power, only an alternative prospect of self resolution. You can use that knowledge to make decisive choices knowing that though fate may intervene, destiny is always of your own making.'

'You are right, Mrs Henderson, I've been a fool most of my life, thinking that it was what others thought that should guide my life, I realise now that come what may, live or die, it must be by my own hand. I see it now, that my destiny belongs to me; my choices should be mine to create the most from the opportunities I have been given and so often refused or ignored. Please continue Mrs Henderson, is there more the cards can share with us?'

'There are four more cards to turn John, I'll go and put the kettle on again while you consider if you really want to know what else they have to say. . .' Rowena smiled, stood and wandered happily into the kitchen, time for another well earned cuppah and perhaps a biscuit too.

**

'Until you said what you said Mrs Henderson,' began John, on Rowena's return, 'it would never have occurred to me that there was ever a choice here. I've thought about it, deeply too, in such a short while, I don't need to see these other cards, I can probably predict what they will say. I'll enjoy that cup of tea and a biscuit with you; pay you for your time and be on my way. I thank you greatly for your help; I already sense that at last I will be free.'

'You are most welcome John, you and the cards of fate have shared a journey of discovery together; They have shown you a direction and now you are on your own again. . . but I suspect, no longer lost.'

The china cups chinked once more in their saucers and the room felt good.

Two weeks later, Rowena was at work in the care home, tidying the empty day room when she noticed a local newspaper opened on a page that straightway caught her eye. She knew that man in the photograph; sure enough it was John!

She had been right, it wasn't his real name; he was in fact, Robert Hughs-Creighton the long lost son of Sir David Hughs-Creighton, Earl of Oakscombe.

Rowena picked up the newspaper and with only one thought on her mind sank deep into one of the comfy chairs. She began to read:

JOY RETURNS TO THE MANOR
Son and heir returns from the dead.

Robert Hughs-Creighton, long lost son of Earl David Hughs-Creighton and who disappeared some ten years ago when aged 22, has last Tuesday night returned home to the joyful arms of his father.

A close family friend told our reporter, 'We all thought he was dead but here he is fit and well and large as life. When Robert's mother committed suicide after a long mental illness he was away at university. We never saw him again and not a word did we hear from anyone, despite extensive efforts by the Earl. Without any contact, David feared the worst and the Manor has been a very sad place for many years now. Tuesday evening late, the Earl answered a resolute knock on his door and there stood Robert, it was such a happy reunion, I can't tell you how much it means to friends and family to have the dear boy back home.'

The Echo's own Janie Simson managed to have a few words with the prodigal son himself and he had this to say.

'I'd like to say sorry to all those to whom I may have caused concern, it was never my intention. I merely followed my heart and while learning much about life at university it beckoned me to a new world and a new love. Nothing from then went well for me, life became one tortuous struggle and conflict hunted me out daily. I began to fear I would follow in my good mother's footsteps and returned to this, my home town, to make my final peace with the world. In my moment of indecision, fate showed me a fortune teller's advert. It was a card that called to me like my mother called to me when I was young. I followed and listened; I shall be ever grateful for the wisdom and guidance I was given. So begins my life anew, this time I shall waste nothing. I thank you all for your time and understanding.'

Rowena let the newspaper fall to her lap and leant back in the chair. 'Should I too go home?' she wondered.
'Tonight I'll light that candle and read the cards just for me,' she smiled, 'and then we'll see, won't we?'

**

'Rather light a candle than complain about the darkness.'

IS IT THE DRUM OR THE
DRUMMER THAT LIVES ON?

Susie was in her mid to late forties I suppose, although she had an ever childlike sense of adventure which constantly led her to seek out all manner of strange and alternative lifestyles.

Susie's patient and contented older husband, Daniel, a retired police inspector, often joked that it must be in her blood and that in previous lives she was a witch – probably burnt at the stake. He repeated this to her one day when she returned from a past life regression sitting she'd just had as a birthday treat. Dan didn't mind her peculiar interests, they did nobody any harm. If they did, of course it would be different, very different.

'Well,' she smiled with arms in mock akimbo, 'it wasn't like that at all – well, not quite anyway.' Susie continued, 'Some of the things that came up have raised my interest in my own past, you know, ancestors and the like. You could help me with that Dan; it would be easy for you. Now, how would you like a nice cup of tea and a big slice of carrot cake?'

Dan laughed; to be sure his younger wife kept him entertained as well as on his toes. 'We'll start tomorrow, just you be prepared to find witches somewhere back there! Now where's my tea?'

Due greatly to his previous employment, Dan was an absolute ace at tracing the family history, he was logical and methodical in maintaining accurate records and he kept an open mind about any possibilities that others might miss. Despite both Susie's parents having passed away and creating a difficult starting point, in less than two weeks he'd mapped out a chart of Susie's family tree, including lots of intriguing extra details extracted from certificates and census returns. One evening he called Susie to the kitchen where the impressive chart laid spread on the table.

'There,' he said triumphantly, tapping with the point of his trusty retirement gift pen on a name he'd written a little way up the page, 'this is what you need, a living relative that might tell you first hand of your past.'

Susie looked at him bemused; she had long thought any family was either dead or had emigrated into obscurity.

'Yes Susie, this lady here,' tapping the name again, 'is your great aunt Evelyn, and this is her address. Amazingly she doesn't live too far away. Why not give her a telephone call on this number and see if she'll meet with you,' a very satisfied Dan put down his pen with a smile and a flourish and handed Susie a neatly annotated slip of paper.

Susie was lost deep in thought and held the piece of paper close to her heart for nearly an hour before she made the call. Once contact was made, it was as though they had known each other all their lives. In a moment's meeting, two total strangers had melted together as if of one mind.

'Oh, Susie dear, you must be Helen's little girl, how lovely to speak with you, you must be all grown up now. You must come and visit as I can't get about as much as I used to you know. I'll have something special waiting for you.'

They arranged that Susie would visit the very next Saturday afternoon, 'it's the last house in the cul-de-sac, I'm afraid the paintwork needs doing. . . it's the big house on your right with attic windows. I'll leave the front door open for you,' Evelyn explained.

Saturday came soon enough and on Susie's insistence Dan joined her. Just as Evelyn had said, the large old house looked worse for wear, as did the unkempt garden; Dan could see that no work had been carried out for many years; he hoped that Evelyn was still able to live comfortably inside.

In a back room, brightly lit through large sash windows, they sat on oak dining chairs around a finely varnished oak dining table on which Evelyn had placed various items of family interest.

'Could you bring the tea through dear?' she said to Dan, pointing towards the open kitchen door, 'I'm afraid I'd drop it if I try.'

Evelyn still had all her marbles so to speak, but was somewhat frail now and hadn't slept in the upper floors for many years. As they settled down around the table with their tea, Evelyn showed various documents that she'd inherited, she and Susie shared the same ancestors and the common bond was overtly tangible.

'You'll be interested in this chap, Susie dear,' Evelyn grinned, sliding across a sepia photograph of an eccentric professor like gentleman who appeared to be posing in an antique shop.

'Was this his shop then, Aunt?' questioned Susie.

'Why, no dear, this was taken in his house – he was a great collector of all manner of extraordinary objects. . . some of them quite strange to be sure. He was a well travelled man and at one time worked for one of the great universities – that is until peculiar things began to happen, then they retired him. Stress they said it was. . . gave him a small pension. Nevertheless, I think they were increasingly uncomfortable with him rambling on about voices he heard in his head. Well, I mean, nobody else heard them, did they? He was a nice man, Hugh was his name and he'd likely be an uncle to your own grandfather. . . ,' Evelyn stopped suddenly to listen. They'd all heard it, it was a sort of bumping noise, not easy to describe.

'Perhaps that's him now,' joked Dan.

Evelyn smiled at him, 'No, I don't think so dear, that happens a lot, I think it's a loose window or door upstairs and it knocks when the wind blows, I've not been up there for years now and can't even remember the last time I was in the attic.'

'I'll check it out before we go Evelyn, just make sure it's all safe and secure for you,' promised Dan with believable authority.

'While you're up there dear, would you do me a great favour? Before he died, Hugh left me an item that he said should be passed on. On no account was I to either throw it away or give it to someone outside the family. Mind you, it didn't come from our family in the first place. It was one of his special collectables from a trip he made to Canada. Being a strange chap, in the nicest possible meaning of the word of course, he quickly made some good friends who were descendants of the Native American community. They were Shamans or something, whatever that means, of the Dakota tribe, or at least I think that's what he said. I haven't any children Susie, you are my only living relative and I'd like you to have it. No, it's much more than that, I think that you were always meant to have it, don't ask me why.'

Evelyn certainly liked to talk but Susie and Dan were enjoying it – for them this was all exciting stuff.

'So what is it I should look for?' asked Dan.

'Silly me, of course, I didn't say, did I? I must be getting daft in my old age. It's a thinnish hide covered drum, bigger than a dinner plate and has a faint image of a wolf and full moon on the front. . . I think at some time Hugh wrote some words on the back. It's very dusty up there, you be careful how you go,' Evelyn was still talking as Dan left the room to explore his way to the attic.

Dan carefully checked all doors and windows on the way up to see if they were loose fitting enough to make that knocking noise – none were. The attic was truly a proper attic in the old style; fully boarded out and with plaster walls, it had a number of curtainless casement windows and its well fitting entrance door was reached by a sturdy timber staircase.

It was indeed very dusty in the attic and not without a few old cobwebs either. It had the appearance of being at one time a pleasant living room but had slowly descended into use as a storage space. Dan checked all the windows for security, thinking as he did, that Evelyn probably had little idea any more just what was in this old attic. Putting it down to his old police instincts, Dan was drawn to a chest of drawers covered by an old blanket over in the far corner. On investigating further Dan realised there was something under the blanket and, lifting it carefully, was thrilled to find what he'd been sent to fetch, the drum. It was in much better condition than he'd expected, in fact, it seemed as though someone had been looking after it for all those years. As Dan picked up the drum he couldn't resist giving it a couple of gentle taps with his open hand. He knew immediately that Susie would fall in love with it at first sight. With a final and confident check of the door as he left, Dan returned with both excitement and anticipation to the drawing room downstairs.

'We heard you find the loose door, which one was it?' Evelyn asked.

Dan just nodded and told her that they were all fine now and he doubted she'd be hearing the noises again.

Susie didn't notice any of the conversation at all; she was completely mesmerised by the drum, it seemed that spirit and imagination were connecting her to it. . . and the art work, well, how beautifully done, if the wolf and the moon didn't look real enough then Susie didn't know what did.

As they stood at the front door step with hugs and goodbyes, a shaking and frail Evelyn explained how fortuitous their meeting was, 'Don't ask me how or why I think this but I believe you were meant to have this drum and that somehow all those years ago Hugh knew that you would find it through me one day. You found me just in time too as this house has become too much of a burden and soon I'm moving into a nursing home, not sure exactly when as the doctor is organising it. I'll let you know what happens. God bless you both and safe journey, enjoy the drum won't you. . . remember what Hugh said.'

They waved from the car windows and drove slowly away with some now very mixed feelings about the visit, joy at the meeting, excitement about the drum and worry about Evelyn's health. They were never to hear from her again, only to read about her in the obituary column. That was a sad day; A quiet day for reflection on their short but poignant encounter that would change both their lives forever.

Sadness couldn't last though, not while Susie had the drum. She'd tried to read Hugh's writing on the back but time had faded the ink, Dan also tried, 'Sorry Susie I can't read it either,

I'm afraid it's destined to be as much a mystery as Hugh himself.'

Several months later, Susie had discovered much about the drum; it was like a portal into a dream world of another reality.

'Not going to your Yoga thing tonight, then Susie?' enquired Dan as he prepared for watching a European Cup match on TV later that evening.

'No, they don't understand what I've been saying, they're too backward thinking now for me,' she replied, 'I've told them about the messages I hear from the drum and they act like it's silly, like it can't be true.'

'That damned drum,' thought Dan trying not to show it but he'd had just about enough of it himself. 'No wonder she can't go to any of her groups anymore - I'm fed up with her ramblings myself.'

'Perhaps you should just keep the drum and your dreams to yourself at the meetings, Susie,' advised Dan.

She snapped back sharply, 'Don't you start either,' and stormed off to the other room to play the drum for guidance.

Whenever she beat the drum she entered a strangely spiritual but yet more earthy and mesmerising world - a world of far off places, mystical people, wild nature and voices; voices that had messages for her. Sometimes she would feel another pair of hands playing the drum at the same time as she, but the other player was so much better, more emotive, more spiritual; more like the drum was speaking its wisdom in its own language. On occasion, in this other world, she saw the old white wolf loping in the moonlight to the edge of a camp site, smoke drifting from the tepees quietly into the night sky to join the camp fires of the ancestors. Her fingers would beat the drum yet she would feel nothing, it was as though she wasn't there; her body was still in the room but her spirit had already left. She knew in wakeful moments that she lost awareness of her body because consciousness had left it. It was so exciting, it made sense of all she had learned before but at a level deeper than any of her old teachers could ever have explained. She would never let the drum go. . . she was certain that now she knew just how Hugh must have felt, sometimes she even thought she sensed his presence. At times, when the wolf would visit the Indian camp, she became aware of herself calling out to it in a strange language. 'Anaahey, anaahey,' she would cry to the old white wolf; it seemed so right to welcome a friend in such manner. So many times she sensed that she had become a wolf, she knew how it felt to stand in a wolf's body – how else could she know this?

Susie initiated these amazing experiences by first entering a quiet place in her mind and allowing her hands to beat the drum in whatsoever fashion they would chose for themselves. Many times Susie realised that the skill of the drummer was coming through her and not from her – it was a skill far beyond her conscious understanding and ability. At times the drum beat sounded to her hearing mind like the thundering hooves of some great beast with pounding heart carrying her spirit on some mystical errand in a far off land and time.

Though the white wolf did not always appear, the more Susie beat the drum and entered the spirit world the more she saw patterns emerge. The white wolf often arrived at the edge of the camp in winter and each time during that season's full moon the white wolf and companions would howl their song of hunger. By now Susie knew for sure that the spirit people she was joining were shamans, just as there were many things that simply became 'known' to her – they knew what it felt like to be the wolf, to run like the wolf, to think like the wolf. They knew how every effortless muscle felt, when they rubbed their necks on a tree they felt the fur on bark – their spirits, being one with the wolf, knew no fear. Her spirit left her body and she hunted the snow clad timber line for deer with the pack – there was no telling reality from dream world, each place had its own sense of being and truth. When Susie returned to her body, she knew where she had been - the knowing was still with her, so much so that even when fully conscious and aware she could still sense the powerful connected movement of the wolf's muscles. How else could she know how a wolf ran, if she hadn't been one?

As the years wore on so did the strain on their relationship and eventually Susie and Dan agreed to go their separate ways. He moved back to his home town and Susie stayed as she was.

Dan plodded on in a simple life of retirement and he renewed old acquaintances from the force. One Christmas he was invited to a reunion party. . . 'How's the lovely Susie?' an old friend asked.

'Long story,' Dan replied, 'short answer is I don't know. She became fixated, addicted almost, to some sort of cult like thing – just needed to go her own way. It's a great shame but there are no guarantees in life old pal.'

'Only the one,' added his friend, smiling, 'only the one,' and patted Dan kindly on the shoulder in sympathy.

Meanwhile, as the years sneaked by unnoticed until they were well past, Susie continued to discover more and more while on her out of body journeys. It was beyond her understanding why others weren't queuing up to do the same; it wasn't as though she'd kept her discoveries a secret, just that they didn't seem to want to know. Susie lost all contact with the therapy community which she had frequented so much before and she spent more time alone, though not spiritually alone of course. At one point she'd been writing engaging articles for a holistic health magazine under the nom-de-plume of 'Moon Wolf.' As her writings (or wild ravings as the editor eventually began to view them) became more intense, the magazine refused any further submissions from her. Susie began to spend more time talking to herself, her drum and the spirits that visited. Susie had never studied Canadian history nor that of the First Nation peoples but now she knew so much of it, the knowledge just seemed to turn up, much like finding hidden treasure in the attic of her mind. Much of what she knew was never of the written word but came from fable and song. She just seemed to 'know' without looking or asking.

She knew all the stars where ancestors had found a greater peace from an ever alienating world. She knew about the Moon, its influence on intuition and how it guarded the earth while the Sun rested. Susie may have known all of this, but not a word of Dan's death; he who'd shared the joys in life and had been so instrumental in Susie's fate.

As the years steadily grew into decades, Susie's house and garden also began to fall into decline and she spent ever more time visiting the spirit world while her earthly body became increasingly frail. One day, she picked up the drum and turned it to look on the inside; it wasn't something she'd ever been bothered with before as the wolf and the moon were far more alluring. By now Susie had no contacts in the 'normal' world and not one living relative of whom she was aware, she'd abandoned the family history research when she found the pleasure of the drum and now she was alone. To Susie's great surprise, Hugh's writing and some hitherto unnoticed strange symbols were becoming clearer, the older and more frail she became the clearer the writing. Finally, using her reading glasses and in good light, she could at last read Hugh's message.

'I have at last deciphered the ancient symbols, they foretell a mystical journey. A journey entirely of your free will to make but you must confer the drum to another before death summons you. Failure has grave consequences. When my writing becomes clear enough to read, please hurry, you will have little time left. May the spirits be with you, Hugh.'

Hugh's writing finally delivered its stark but belated warning. As so often happens in life, a warning which often condemns us to wander a path we had mistakenly chose to follow. The wonders of hindsight arrive too late to serve us well in our time of need.

However, Susie did try to find another who would accept the drum as their own but without success; in part she didn't want to be free of it, its hold too strong for her weaker will.

Susie reflected on her dilemma, could she ask the old white wolf? The white wolf symbolised intelligence, leadership, family and strength; the white wolf also epitomised perseverance and intuition. The question was, 'Where were these qualities in her, what was she doing wrong?'

Susie knew the ancestors around their starlight camp fires better than she knew who ran the corner shop down her street. She knew the life of bear, eagle and deer better than she did her neighbours of more than thirty years. She actually liked it that way.

Late one cold winter's evening at the time of the full moon, Susie was not feeling very well, she had been ailing for a while but now the pain in her chest and joints was becoming intolerable. Susie chose to leave her pain racked body behind and visit the spirits through the drum's mystical portal. She placed lighted candles all about the room, drew the curtains and turned off the electric light, then settled into her comfortable chair and began her ritual.

**

As she arrived at the spirit camp she noticed it was more crowded than usual, as though the shamans were gathering for a special occasion, there were many camp fires and several faces she had not seen before. Looking up she could clearly see the full moon, seemingly smiling down on her like a long lost sister just found. The camp was surrounded by a low lying evening mist among the nearby Alders and Maples. As she peered into the mist she saw not one wolf but two, one light, one dark. As her eyes grew accustomed to the mist she saw the great grizzly bear and the black bear too. . . oh, and deer present in plenty; at their head was a great and noble stag, an ancient looking beast of wisdom with a greying white coat. Susie became ever excited as the mist further revealed what it so recent had concealed. The mists for Susie were clearing; the camp was circled with the benevolent gaze of animals and spirits, all looking on in expectation.

An elder and obviously revered shaman beckoned her to sit with him at his fire; she sat next to him sensing the welcome he offered, they warmed their hands by the light of the burning wood and watched the sparks of life slowly rise and abandon the fire for another place. As the heat of the fire seemed to warm her very soul, the old shaman told Susie the celebrated tale of the two wolves, one good, one bad. They were opposites in the universe, as must exist for all things and for all time; they would fight each other until the strongest won.

When Susie asked which wolf won – the answer came, 'the one you feed.'

A day later a rubbish skip appeared outside Susie's fire dam-aged house, accompanied by Police tape and a sign that read, 'Keep Clear. Unsafe Structure.'

Three weeks later, the following appeared in the small ads of the local paper:

Genuine Canadian Native Indian Drum.
Endearing and pretty, you'll fall in love with it.
Vibrant and life like art work depicting an elderly squaw
accompanied by a howling wolf under a Full Moon.
Slight smoke damage hence yours for only £20 or near offer.
A bargain you'll not find again in your lifetime.
Tel **** 656768

'Belief gives birth to power.'

THE COIN COLLECTOR

No one would deny, least of all himself, that he was profoundly attached to his coin collection. Not for any monetary value you understand but for an uncanny something else he couldn't really quite explain. He'd had the collection many years, often not even remembering where a particular coin may have been unearthed. Some were the poorer remnants from childhood days when antique shops were known by their proper name - Junk Shops. Oh they were still full of grand and valuable items all right, violins, beautiful framed etchings, mirrors, walking sticks, stamp books of some departed ancient's collection, oil lamps and fine chairs that were once besieged under some plump Edwardian gentleman and there, too, were the coins: jam jars full of coins from around the world and from our past. A few pennies only were enough to buy these treasures; just a few new pennies for lamps of old!

One could never know or even guess where these coins had been before and what they could tell if they could but share their journey's story. Often, when a certain tranquil mood took him, he would fetch the little wooden box from the under-stairs cupboard and remove a coin to investigate further; his coins weren't protected in special folders nor were they labelled and priced. He had sold some once when he was in desperate need of money and thereafter was to know for the rest of his life that they had in fact been priceless to his very soul. Though they were long gone to a professional collector, who had, in hindsight, ruthlessly exacted a somewhat clinical and greedy deal, he had never forgotten those coins; he still felt the pain of their loss. It was almost like they were lost children still calling to him from the grave. Sometimes he told friends of particular treasures he'd known, of Queen Ann, Napoleon, Cromwell, George and Victoria, of copper, silver and gold, of, oh so much he could recall as if only yesterday.

However, one late autumn evening, his ever welcome reunion with the coins would open his eyes and his mind to a whole new world; it could never again be just a box of coins.

He subconsciously picked out a particular coin which seemed to reach out to him as much as he to it; he put away his thoughts of yesteryear and cleaned his magnifying glass with one of those special cloths you find in spectacles cases. Soon the glass sparkled intriguingly in the electric light set above his comfortable chair in the living room.

Within minutes, the living room lights flickered forebodingly and his first thought was another bulb was on its way out; nothing lives for ever, does it? They flickered again, then darkness and silence; the fridge motor he could normally never hear, he now acknowledged by its total absence. He placed the coin in his pocket and, taking small shuffling steps in the dark, walked carefully to the kitchen where he kept a torchlight; it still worked despite the batteries having been in it for at least five years; 'Perhaps some things can live forever,' he thought, marvelling at the lamp's brightness. He checked the circuit board to find nothing had tripped out, 'Must be a local area thing I guess,' he mumbled to himself. Meanwhile, in the light of the torch he spotted some candles on the upper shelf, lovely bee's wax candles he'd bought for a surplus Christmas gift never yet given. 'Oh, lovely, I'd forgotten all about you, you little beauties, come on, you and I can look at the coins together,' he said aloud, it not escaping his attention that he sounded a bit on the eccentric side.

He cleared a place at the pine table in the kitchen, a favourite spot to sit, placed the candle in a little brass holder and lit the flame; it amused his thinking how so much could be achieved with such a tiny spark. He fetched the box and magnifying glass from the living room, returned the torch to its home in the cupboard and taking the chosen coin from his pocket sat on one of the old beech-wood chairs next the candle light.

The magnifying glass was old, nearly as old as he, a gift from his mother for his childhood stamp collection, yet one more thing now lost to the 'never know' land. Some of the stamps had come on letters from America, sent by long ago emigrated relatives of his; they carried a special message. . . and to this day still do. How much he would like to touch one again, an all important stamp placed with loving care to carry a message across the Ocean to family and a land they still loved and never forgot, the land in which their ancestors slept the deep sleep.

'Amazing how caring can lead to lasting,' he thought, then remembered a wonderful pocket knife he'd been given by his grandfather; he'd not had it long before he'd lost it near his father's allotment garden. As he sat at the table lightly resting his hands, he temporarily felt the loss of that precious knife pain him. He didn't know for sure but something in him told him that the knife, an old Jack Knife, was special. It had a large blade on one side and on the other a long spike for getting stones out of horse's hooves; he took a moment to imagine his Grandfather had used this knife in the Great War of 1914, or perhaps the Second World War in 1939. He would never know for sure but something drew the soul in him to think so. On reflection he realised that his soul was still connected in some way to that precious old knife; wherever it was, there was a part of him with it. Who knows, an energy or part of his grandfather's soul still had a connection with it too; Lost in time and space, yet somehow still there, something not ever wanting to let go.

**

He picked up the coin again, a rather interesting bronze coin with crossed rifles on the reverse, it seemed unusually heavy to him and in fact he was finding breathing a little difficult too. 'Strewth,' he mumbled to himself, 'I must be getting old - I certainly feel it tonight.'

In an instant, he could smell burning: wood burning. He jumped up with a start, dropping the coin as he did, sniffing the air keenly and checking the other rooms.

'How damnable odd,' he muttered, half under his breath for there was no sign of fire and nor could he any longer smell burning wood. 'How strange. Don't say old age is giving me hallucinations now.' He inwardly smiled at the possibility, before returning to the kitchen table to continue his studies.

'Thank goodness for these lovely candles,' he thought to himself, having just confirmed that it was a local area blackout by peering through the living room window. Pitch black it was out there, not a light in sight, no Moon, no stars and no passing traffic, just pitch black, he couldn't see a thing out there, almost as if there wasn't.

The candle flame welcomed him back to the kitchen with light, warmth and a strangely mystical presence, though he might deny he felt that, if you were to ask him outright. *(Some things you just don't share for fear of being thought mad, you just keep it to yourself, you know what I mean, don't you?)*

He settled into his pleasurable diversion once more, picked up the coin and placed it in the palm of his left hand. Moving it closer to the light he felt a cold breeze touch him and the candle light flickered wildly, the air was thin and cold like mountain air. . . in shock he dropped the coin on the table and everything returned to normal; he felt normal, breathed easier, the candle flame was relentlessly steady and the room was warm again.

This time he realised that it would be a pointless exercise to check the windows and doors in the house for he now knew that whatever he was experiencing was happening because of the coin, or its energy, or something. He had heard friends talk of such things, they'd told him of those who could touch an object and tell you about the owner and stuff like that, they called it psychot - something or other. He'd never really paid much attention as it all seemed highly improbable to him - at that time anyway!

On this curious and seemingly supernatural evening he decided to give it a try - what had he got to lose?

Composing his nerves and seeking the calmness he'd had at the beginning of the evening, he picked up the coin again. . . nothing! But then, as he relaxed a little more and held the coin closer to the candle light he began to see images. It was most peculiar, on the one hand he could focus on the coin and the candle and then, on the other hand, he could let them fade and watch what we would describe today as a video. He could see mountains, wild rugged mountains, snow clad peaks. He was so excited that he began to think how marvellous this was but the moment he began to think in such a way the images disappeared. He soon learned to stay relaxed and be the observer of what ever would unfold. He was on a truly amazing mind adventure.

Although the room did not overtly change again, he felt the cold mountain air and he smelled the wood smoke from a fire; it wasn't all that clear but he 'saw' a group of strangely dressed men carrying rifles similar to those on the coin. He heard a name called, it sounded a bit like George but not quite, similar though. The rest of the conversation was in a strange language that he knew not but, above all, feelings welled up in him, feelings of honour and justice, hard won by armed struggle, waves of both fear and joy ebbed and flowed in him, the child in the 'seeing,' powerless; the man, victorious.

The imagery faded away but was soon replaced with different people, this time dressed in more modern clothing, it was warmer and the snow had gone but it was the same place. This time there were women also and carrying flowers which they left on the ground, and more talking too; he heard the word 'kleftis' and also what sounded like 'hero.'

It was making more sense now as he became more aware of the context; he was witnessing a family returning to mark a significant monument in their distant family history, about a man who lived long ago, first as a robber then as a national hero.

The people standing there now, talking, singing and leaving the flowers were descendants of this man, the hero, George or Georgius. Feelings of compassion, empathy, connection and pride coursed powerfully through his very being. This commemorative Greek coin must have been up there with them that day on that mountain, carried in one of their pockets; the coin's aura had first absorbed and now it was to impart this experience to a receptive mind, his mind.

The lights in the house flickered once then burned steadily; the fridge motor gently shook itself back to life and mains power restored. The spell was broken for the evening and he gazed thoughtfully at the coin in his hand wondering why he should feel such affinity with such an insignificant and moderately recent Greek coin. He placed it back in the little wooden box and went to put the kettle on.

Glancing at the clock he realised that the power must have been off for about thirty minutes or so, with his cup in hand he returned to the table and blew out the candle. For the life of him he just couldn't remember what had happened in that lost time, not a bit of it.

'Must have slipped off into a day dream. . . it's true, you're just getting old, come on old chap, time for bed,' he said aloud, it not escaping his attention that he sounded a bit on the eccentric side.

**

*'Change the way you look at things,
and the things you look at will change.'*

THE DEVIL'S GEMS?

It was not so very long ago. High up, near an arid plateau of the Chilean Andes, young and yearning hunters of rare gems sought the fortunes of their lives; a hunger encouraged by the insatiable yet glib whims of the well-heeled who inhabit the so-called 'civilised' world.

Lapis Lazuli, like the more common Amethyst, ripped cruelly from the womb of Mother Earth, adorned many a home in Western Europe, frequently in the name of spiritual purification. Gem collectors were everywhere and more than a few used crystals to 'heal the world' safe in the sanctuary of their living rooms. How they were dug up, by whom and for what reason would never enter their heads. It wasn't the world they recognised or inhabited.

**

Propping his well worn shovel against the derelict Ford pickup, Sasha, accompanied by a fleetingly frightened look, coughed up some dust, 'How long have you been here, Max?' he said in a dust croaked eastern European accent.

'Here, at the mine, only about three months but I've been in Chile for a few years now while seeking my fortune; It's not happened yet but my family back home are depending upon my success; they are waiting for my return and to be honest I'd dearly love to go back now but I cannot even afford the cheapest fare,' Max replied with a far off look in his eye, an eye that gazed longingly at a self conjured image of his wife, his two children and aging parents.

The gem mine was high up in the mid Andes, remote from accepted civilisation by two or three difficult days. Their camp, consisting of rudimentary and decaying wooden sheds was set in the appropriately named, 'El Valle del Diablo,' on the northern edge of one of the great plateaus. They were young and all foreigners to Chile, mostly from poor families in Eastern Europe, they all had a smattering of Spanish and a little more than that of English, none of them had any prior mining experience, it was a baptism of fire; a baptism fuelled by a burning desire to strike it rich and then go home as heroes and saviours.

No Chilean nationals would ever work at this particular mine despite their own abject poverty. Villagers always looked on in bewilderment that the foreigners were still alive when occasional visits were forced upon them to a distant village for extra supplies. Few locals would even look at, let alone talk, with them, almost as though they were infected with something dangerous akin to the Black Death and should not be approached. That's what Arek and Egor had said, and being the longest survivors at the mine they should know.

The absent owners weren't thought to be Chilean either; they never came to visit the mine. They were content only to make money out of the infrequent lumps of Lapis Lazuli for which their poorly paid miners had burrowed deep and torn from mother earth with a driven passion. A good find could mean a ticket home; in the beginning they may have had many dreams but it didn't take long for going home to become the sole motive that drove the men to their labours. Going home, leaving Devil's Valley far behind them became the dream.

For the owners it was simply about money, that's all, just money; neither another thought nor care entered their heads. No holiday pay, no holiday even, no safety equipment, no health care and no rest, that's the way it was, take it or leave it. No doubt, if you were to look hard enough, more than a few skeletons would ornament the valley floor. The miners were ensnared by fanciful and no doubt false tales of striking it rich with other gems too, diamonds some said; there was no evidence of this but the hopeful and the poor still cling to every chance they get.

They were running short of water and a delivery was overdue. A young woman called Danita used to deliver supplies and collect any Lapis Lazuli or other stones that the miners had unearthed. She would no longer drive all the way to the camp but would leave everything about half a mile away. It was a struggle for the miners to carry back but as they were so glad to see it, the burden was almost one of joy and in any event a welcome short break from their lung wrenching and back breaking daily grind. At one time before the present arrangements, when supplies were delivered into the camp itself, Danita had taken a fancy to one of the miners, she was often seen watching him and smiling; until the dusty cough began. It was almost as though there was no point in loving a dead man walking. Danita had turned away so as not to watch any more suffering and that was the last time she and the supplies came all the way to the huts.

'Haven't any women ever been here as miners then, Egor?' enquired Sasha.

'Yes Sasha, there was one once; a strong young adventurous woman called Katrina as I recall. They seem to be more sensitive than us men, more intuitive I guess. Anyway, she said the place gave her the creeps and that she'd rather die in poverty than sell her soul in such a place for a few dollars. That was it . . . she just left, never heard from her again,' replied Egor, as his almost lifeless eyes stared out across an even more lifeless valley.

Two days later they all walked down to the supply drop, the rocks that they had left there were gone, collected to swell the coffers of the mine owner, known only to them by the alias of 'Esteban'; They reckoned only God and his mother knew Esteban's real identity, it was a shady, cut throat business finding and selling Lapis, in all probability illegally sold abroad to the highest bidders. No doubt there were many disagreeable characters who'd like to pick up the gems for free without having to crawl about for years in some dust ridden death pit they called a mine. Neither would there be any doubt that the Chilean government had a vested interest in preventing the smuggling of precious resources with not a peso paid in tax.

The day before they collected the supplies, they had made a good find, a truly exceptional find, almost a barrow full of superb quality Lapis Lazuli all within a pocket of loose earth and rock. It had been curiously easy to locate, as if someone had mined there before and had stashed it close by for them to discover. What a happy day; and now as they returned with their supplies it was yet another of their infrequent happy days. Tired in body but with minds wide awake, bursting with excitement and hope, they planned to celebrate that evening.

The Sun was setting and the mountain air grew cold with the wind that arrived like clockwork at that time of evening. The men retired to one of the sheds and it was not long before a Primus oil stove warmed the air and cooked their meal, creating a peculiar aroma of burning paraffin and spices. It wasn't long before they had all eaten and eaten well, as was their habit on the first day of fresh food, though their meals dwindled to pauper's handouts as the day of the next longed for delivery slowly approached. They were too tired to clean up straightaway and just sat around wherever they could make themselves comfortable.

Egor beamed with pleasure and announced, 'I have a surprise for you all, something to wash the Devil's dust away.' He produced a large bottle of vodka from his rucksack. 'This has been waiting a long time in here to see the light of day, I hope as keen to see the light as we are when we leave the mine,' he laughed, mixed with a little irksome cough. Now they all sat up and leaned forward, this was an unexpected treat.

'Aha! Stalychnia Vodka, a good one, where did you get this from old friend?' exclaimed an excited Arek, for whom not a drop of alcohol had passed his lips since leaving the motherland; this was going to be a pleasure. Rough hands wiped their cups clean and their outstretched arms met the free flowing and generous bottle.

'Cheers!' 'Nastrovia!' 'To our success!' 'To our great find and to our health!' The toasts came thick and fast, cups chinked together. The mountain air and the long period of abstinence made for a potent combination and soon the toasts became longer and the drinking slower. Voices slurred and minds fantasised.

They looked at their barrow of Lapis. Even in the dim light the quality shone through, 'What do you think it's worth Egor?' asked Max brushing some dinner remnants off his front on to the earth floor.

'Oh, very much, very much, enough to get us all home if we sold it ourselves; to the right buyer this is worth thousands of dollars. See, some pieces have little gold flecks - worth even more. This was a very special find, it was fate that we should find it,' Egor put the stone back in the barrow and raised his cup again; 'A toast. A toast to fate I say.'

Their cups chinked yet again and all as one the cry went up, 'To fate!'

All went quiet as they finished the last of the vodka and each wistfully contemplated their destiny.

'Why don't the local people dig these stones themselves, why leave it to us?' wondered Sasha out loud.

Egor shifted on the sacking cover of the crate on which he sat, he leant forward and speaking quietly as though confiding a great secret and inherently not wishing anyone, or anything, outside the shed to overhear, 'Oh they do dig for gems, and there are many, many good Chilean miners all over this country, but not here, not in 'El Valle del Diablo.' It's all part of myth and legend; they say that Devil's Valley is so called because the Devil himself is mining here. We are mining downwards and old Diablo is mining upwards, the locals fear to dig here in case they meet him coming the other way.' Egor paused for effect in his story but also because his vodka infused friends, all strong young men, not much afraid of anything were falling about laughing at the thought.

'Pity he's not here now for a drink!' shouted Sasha.

'He's too late now' reposted Max, 'it's all gone!'

They all laughed heartily again and felt their collective spirit grow in power.

Egor put his cup down and continued in his secretive tone, 'Local legend has it that the Devil is angry that Lapis Lazuli is seen by us mere mortals as the colour for the Gods, the colour of vision and spirit. Angels are painted wearing this colour, a royal and honourable colour and old Diablo is angry; he seeks to bury the stone deep, making it difficult to find and dangerous to mine or even own. You'll have noticed that we all have that tiresome cough, the cough is a sign of ailing health, a hint that death, and perhaps the Devil, is waiting close by. Where do you think all the previous miners went? Home with their pockets full of riches? Does this look like such a place to you?' he asked, waving an open palm around the shed's obvious display of wretched poverty.

Arek interrupted, 'but we found a whole barrow of the stuff, all together, it was easy.'

'I suspect too easy,' replied Egor who had always been known for his sceptical thinking, then adding in way of jest, 'perhaps old Diablo found these stones first and was just keeping them there. . . or worse still, he wanted us to find them.'

Feeling fortified from the good food and plentiful vodka, Max stood and invited his comrades to do the same, 'Let's fill in the mine, stop the Devil getting out, take the stones; we owe 'Esteban' nothing. We go to Santiago, sell the stones and share the prize - then we all go home.' With unified grunts of drunken approval they strode purposefully across the bright moonlit ground, shovels in hand to the waiting spoil heaps.

With childlike excitement they toiled ceaselessly through the night, it was so much easier to fill the mine in than it had been to dig it out; the thought of going home re-energized them with the strength that earlier months of despair had stolen from them. Dawn came and in the light of the rising Sun they brushed the Devil's dust from their clothes and coughed it from their lungs. Taking what they needed from the shed the four young adventurers set off on their long journey home.

It is said that only three of them survived the long and painful trip to Santiago and no one knows if any ever made it all the way home; what we do know is that by then, weak, hungry and powerless they sold the Lapis for a lamentably paltry sum, it was all they could wring from the corrupt gem dealers of the market.

Their exceptionally high grade Lapis was cut, polished and sold on to Europe where it found new homes at great expense. The true value of the stones can never be known but their cost can.

One gentleman had a beautiful pendant made as a gift for his wife, it cost him the proverbial arm and a leg to buy and he was very disappointed when she stopped wearing it.

'I'm sorry dear,' she'd said, 'but it seems to give me a cough every time I wear it.'

All across the land, in shops, dresser drawers, shelves and cupboards the stones are waiting for you to inherit or buy; waiting patiently to fulfil the Devil's dream.

Of course,
I don't believe a single
word of it. . .
It's just some old wives tale,
isn't it?

(Some of the author's ancestors were miners, mostly for coal or iron ore. At least three died in pit accidents, two more suffered from silicosis and struggled to breathe for the rest of their lives.

The author himself, as a potholer, has entered closed down iron ore mines (illegally) and as an active fire-fighter was well acquainted with the hazards of carcinogenic dusts and of confined places.)

**

'What we deeply cling to imprisons us.'

THE SHIFTING SANDS OF ETERNITY.

Despite the timeless beauty of this wild and isolated site, something uncanny had infected it with inexplicable foreboding. It is easiest understood as a short stretch of deserted and rather obscure coastline, similar in nature to the Solway Firth that separates England from Scotland but smaller, more remote, poorly defined on the map and avoided with a passion by the few locals who lived inland nearby.

Not too many souls had ever walked those constantly shifting sands of the Van Hades estuary. It was so named after an adventuring 15th century Dutch sailing ship that ran aground with the loss of all crew. It was said that none of the crew were ever found. . . either alive or dead.

Local legend has it that the foundered crew's bodies had been swallowed up by the shifting sands, along with the ship and some bizarre cargo; the spirit of which bound the hapless crew for all eternity to keep it safe from inquisitive eyes. Nothing had ever been found along the sands to substantiate such stuff of myth and legend; treasure seekers and archaeologists alike who had explored the area never seemed to leave any clues as to what if anything they might have discovered. Almost as though they had never been there in the first place. Twice a day the rushing tide would wipe nature's slate clean again; all debts paid. However, that which lingered deep underneath lay still, just biding its time, waiting patiently.

A curious twist of geological fate had created a barrier of sandstone cliffs along the shoreline that ran to the west of the river mouth. Beyond the river to the East, great sand dunes and a tangled forest of wind-strewn trees buried from sight the insanely religious hamlet of Dugenen, some four miles distant.

Our visitor was alone. Nondescript and simply dressed, he was of medium build with blue grey eyes and carried a pensive expression that seemed to age him beyond his years. He had alighted from the irregular and erroneously named once weekly 'market day' bus that was supposed to serve the remote local community. He'd left the bus at his own request and to the utter bewilderment of the driver just past the small stone bridge that crossed the Dugenen river; Oh, don't bother to look, you'll not find it marked on the map; just one more peculiarity of the area, it's a place which few seek to visit and even fewer return.

For some reason far beyond any of his own, he was drawn by an inner longing to visit this isolated westerly coast and he soon found himself meandering along its gently undulating desert of sands between cliff and sea. Strangely, something within him felt at home there, yet, until the yearning to visit came over him, he had never even heard of the place.

He'd told no one of his plans, for in truth he knew almost no one to tell. He'd lost touch with old work colleagues and social contacts when he'd wholeheartedly embraced some quasi spiritual group who, almost cult like, believed in and experimented with reincarnation rituals. His experiments, mainly with non registered 'fringe' therapists, with past life regressions and other similar activities were all a bit much for his old friends who had simply left him to his own devices. . . 'He seems happier that way,' 'he's not his old self anymore,' 'he's missing out on life, can't understand what he sees in it,' they'd confided in each other as the mutual abandonment grew deeper still.

He'd always felt he'd been born at the wrong time, he felt that he belonged in a different time and place, modern life just didn't feel right to him; he was out of his depth.

The beach was wide and in places very flat, an obvious warning to the wary that any incoming tide would be fast, faster they say than a galloping horse. The sands varied in hue from light to dark, from gold to ochre, and some was forever wet from water that wept like mournful tears from the sandstone cliffs. Cliffs that for some unknown reason sank a well of fear deep within his being. He looked away from them immediately and felt a little better as he continued westwards towards the sinking Sun.

Some way along the shoreline and now out of sight of the forest that hid the village, he was amazed to see footprints in the sand. They were going his way too; 'They seem to be that of a man, barefoot and not in a particular hurry,' he reflected. Perhaps that was why he was drawn to add his own presence there, perhaps he was destined to meet this person and discover answers to his neurotic eternal questions on life's journey. Was this one of those synchronistic coincidences of which he'd learned so much while on an advanced psyche regression event near Dartmoor?

The bright light of the lowering Sun and the knowledge that someone else was out there on the beach before him tempted him willingly further. Meanwhile at his back, a moonless night stalked him like one of Satan's hounds, steadily dark and silent from the East. At one point he thought he heard a voice and stopped to listen, the wet shifting sand willingly moving out of the way as his good shoes sank to the ankles. He could not place the location of the voice, which seemed to him to be coming quite frantic. Even more peculiar was that the voice was not of his own native English tongue. It oddly didn't matter though as he seemed to understand the meaning behind the words if not the actual words themselves.

He looked at the footprints in the soft wet sand, they were going deeper now and who ever it was that left them was now in a hurry, the footprints were further apart and scuffing in the sand at the toes indicated something of a purposeful run. As he took off his own shoes the sand seemed to welcome his feet as though they were old friends come home after a long absence, then he too began to run, his own feet matching the lengthening strides of whoever it was that had gone before him. It was like following a ghost; though the footprints were fresh, as hard as he tried he could not catch up and yet still on occasion would hear that almost familiar but now desperate voice again. 'God behoede ons, de zee de zee !'

At times he seemed to lose contact with himself, or at least who he have thought he might have been earlier that day; on occasion as he returned to what we might think of as his normal mind he was increasingly disturbed to see his rapidly lengthening shadow desperately reaching back behind him into the gathering eastern gloom; reaching back as if it wished to abandon him and return to the road, the village, its people, the bridge and safety. . . however, it was all too late for that now; time and tide indeed wait for no man, already any thought of return was without hope; assuredly, he had taken a step too far. He began to be acquainted with his new found fear intimately and he angrily cursed himself for throwing away everything in life on such a foolhardy and ill thought-out whim. How stupid he had been.

It was too late to turn back; there was no going back. He seemed on a one way trip to hell and he must now find another way out. He could only hope the frightful sandstone cliff would change to dunes or be lower or climbable or anything but what they were. His fear and desperation drove him blindly on to run even harder, oblivious now that his footprints matched not only in stride but in exactitude the footprints in the softening depths of the shifting sand. . . they were as if his very own.

Part of him felt he was going home to be reunited with one who had gone before and part of him felt that his very soul was being torn from the life he could have had and still enjoyed for years to come. The silent sandstone cliffs stood sentinel and watched impassively; the incoming tide rushed past his ankles as if in a hurry not to stay and watch; the harder he struggled the deeper he sank; the sands were soft but gripped him with a power he could never resist; as his body sank to chest height in the liquid sand his tortured being screamed out in English.

'No, no, I don't want to die. . . God help me. . . help me, help me please. . . '

Yet still, one other in him simply smiled an old sailor's smile and quietly said, 'Hallo oude vriend we ontmoeton elkar weer.'

**

None would hear his wretched pleas for help, so quickly stifled by sea and sand.

Early evening stars looked quietly down and saw nothing but the gentle waves lapping peacefully against the cliffs. The stalwart sandstone cliffs kept their stony silence. The shifting sands of eternity welcomed yet one more of the ill-fated or simply curious deep into its bosom.

Some day in some new life he may be back again, perhaps he'll live in our town, perhaps we'll meet him, or perhaps one of us is him.

Next time you walk the estuary sands please take care, won't you?

**

Translations:
'God behoede ons, de zee de zee!' (*'God protect us, the sea the sea!'*)
'Hallo oude vriend we ontmoeton elkar weer.' (*'Hello old friend, we meet again.'*)

**

'Tomorrow does not exist - it never did.'

GOING HOME AGAIN
A YOUNG MINER'S TALE.

An autumn darkness arrived unexpectedly early that evening at the humble farm cottage, as Henry lit the oil lamp and thoughtfully put the last of their coal on the fire. 'That's the last the world will see of that wee lump of coal,' he muttered, under his breath.

The significance of loss and coal was particularly poignant to Henry whose father had been killed in a mining disaster many years previously. 'Dust explosion they said,' mumbled Henry, reliving the day he heard that sad news. He watched fleeting sparks of coal dust flash across the dwindling fire.

'What was that dear?' asked Martha, his caring wife of some twenty five years.

'Nothing Martha, just mumbling about the last of the coal. It'll be early to bed I reckon tonight. There's damp in the air for sure,' replied Henry, hiding his real feelings once more, it's what men did back then.

Though born into a mining family, Henry was encouraged by his late father, James Richmond, to seek different employment; something cleaner and away from the near slavery to which miners were still subjugated in Victorian times. Brave men all, their families too who often worked underground with them; brave men all with scant recognition ever given by the wealthy mine owners. It seemed it was their lot in life, indeed their fate, in service to the Empire of the day.

Henry had taken his father's advice and moved south to become a farm labourer; he would not see his father alive again. Henry found a fine young woman from the Henderson family to marry; she was a domestic servant also a long way from home and they met at a hiring fair in the nearby market town.

To be honest it was still a poor life but at least it was free of the choking grime of the pits.

Henry and Martha had but only one child, a boy they called James. James was an adventurous soul. One of his regrets was being too young to enlist for the First World War, by the time he was old enough it was over thank God. He remained disappointed at having lost the chance to escape the abject poverty of life as a farm labourer. James had watched his parents work so hard for so little. There they were now, huddled by a tiny fire and with precious little food in their bellies to keep them warm and well.

Wind-blown rain tapped like an impatient visitor on the small cottage window as if to make an announcement but it was James, standing by the mantle's edge, who spoke, 'Father, Mother. . . I have something important to tell you. I have made up my mind and you will not dissuade me.'

In the 'before their age' tiredness of their faces, he could see that they already knew what he was about to say. They had often wondered when the day would come, for as like death, come it does.

'In the morning I leave for Scotland. In Lanarkshire they are employing miners to dig for coal. I want to be a miner, like my grandfather. . . I feel it in my blood to follow in his footsteps.' He tried to make it sound like his only reason for leaving. The truth was, he was a drain on his parents; he was an extra mouth they couldn't afford to feed. He knew that in the past his mother had pretended that she had already eaten earlier so that her son could have a meal. He'd seen his father limp and struggle with labouring that was all but beyond his ability to survive. The farmer wasn't a bad man but like most landowners of the time was exceedingly frugal with the wages of servants. The very reason the middle classes could afford them – they were cheap and easily disposable; many would find a pauper's grave on common ground.

Henry and Martha knew they must accept James' decision and the three of them sat by their last fire together and exchanged words of advice, wisdom and comfort.

Later as Martha and Henry lay shivering in a cold and uncomforting bed, their minds savaged by the impending loss of their only son, Martha spoke, 'In the morning we must smile and be happy for him though it breaks our hearts, we will give him what ever money we can find and make sure he knows he can come home as many times as he likes. . . and he must write us and let us know how he is. . . we don't want him being a stranger.'

Henry hid a deep sigh and said with as much fortitude as he could muster, 'We will dear, never fear, we will.'

Morning came with lighter rain than the previous night but James had already left. He'd left early so that darkness would hide his tears, tears for the loss of his family and home, for he could watch them suffer no more. It was now his turn to meet the world alone and find his own destiny, whatever it might bring. He promised himself that he would return one day, yes, he determined he would find great wealth and return to repay his aging parents for all their sacrifice.

A heavy sadness fell like a great stone upon the little cottage. Every night they would dream of James' return. As the years wore on with never a word their dreams became less frequent, more forlorn but not lost forever, no, not lost forever, surely James would return one day.

James had little except coat, boots and dreams to carry away with him on that cold, portentous morning, as he sadly but resolutely walked the nine miles to the Railway station. His ticket was paid for as part of an agreement with the agents employed by the mine owners, to be deducted from his wages. A few other men were waiting at the station; as the great black smoking steam locomotive pulled in and past the short platform, names were called above the noise and those who answered were ushered forward to one of the goods wagons. There was to be no comfort on this journey. The men, now some ten in number excitedly introduced themselves. As the journey wore on the warmth of their meeting was replaced by the cold and hungry reality of their journey. The wooden boards were cold, the only light was through a small dirty window at one end and the only fresh air from a gap in the door to the coupling landing of the wagon.

After a few hours James could stand on his feet no more and, still damp, he wearily slumped against the unrelenting timber walls of the rumbling wagon. For a while the mesmerising, rythmic clickety clack of iron wheels on iron track amused him, until his thoughts were interrupted by a playful nudge on his shoulder.

'Hi mate, my name's er John, John Smith, from London. What's yours?' The voice came from a wiry young man sitting close by, about his own age and with a cheeky grin.

'James, James Richmond, my first time away from home,' he replied with a shiver.

'No worries mate, you'll be fine. You stick with me, I'll see you're alright,' reassured John.

With just a couple of short breaks to take on more coal and water, the train took some ten energy sapping hours to reach a small and dirty station next to a coal marshalling yard.

They were soon jolted out of their dog tiredness by the screeching, rumbling noise of the sliding door and a brutally uncaring demand, 'Come on, off ye's get and look sharp about it, I'm soon awa for ma supper. Quick, quick, make haste. . . ,' it was one of the mine foremen come to walk them to their lodgings.

All the lodgings and houses were owned by the mining company, if you couldn't work in the mine then you couldn't live there. . . simple as that. Everything was owned by the mining company, which in turn was owned by Sir Hubert Montague De Vasey, one of those families that had owned land ever since the Normans invaded. He wasn't a man inclined to visit his mine, his estates in Surrey kept him amused enough.

James, along with John and five others were put up in what looked like an old inn from the outside but inside it was very spartan; wooden boards, big rough dining table with benches and stairs that went up to a number of equally spartan tiny and scantily furnished rooms - their new home.

A little old lady, Helen McLeod her name, a pleasant enough soul but with a voice that commanded instant respect, brought them to attention, 'There's clean water in the wash basin in your rooms. . . keep it like that, I'm not your mother and I'm not here to act like her. The bedding should be clean. . . keep your dirty boots off it and keep it that way, it won't get changed for a month. Breakfast is at five. Don't worry, you'll hear the bell, even the devil himself could hear it. The well is out the side of the hostel, toilets at the back of the yard, you can have a hot bath for two pence in the laundry room by the kitchen. Don't burn all the candles, when you need more you have to buy them yourself at the mine shop.'

James wondered if she was ever going to stop giving orders and if at all he was ever going to remember them. It was so much easier back home. He almost wished he were back there already but John timely slapped him on the back and said, 'Come on James, race you for the best room in the house.'

Mrs McLeod was right about that bell, 'It must be being rung by someone already deaf,' thought James as he eased an aching body out of bed and splashed some cold water on his face. By the time he was downstairs several of the resident miners had already finished their porridge. Mrs McLeod put a bowl in front of him and threw a great ladle of sticky porridge into it, some of it seemed reluctant to leave the safety of the ladle but with a hefty shake it landed solidly in the bowl. James was starving, he'd had nothing to eat for more than a day, and he was so looking forward to the sweet taste of porridge.

'Yuk,' James thought as he screwed up his face, and much out of character angrily demanded, 'Who's put the salt in my porridge?' Even Mrs Mcleod laughed, they all laughed; it was one of the few laughs they ever heard again.

It being their first morning they were to visit the company stores and be provided with suitable clothing and instructions. They had to pay for this too, nothing was free, only the air they breathed, and for many a poor soul there was eventually a terrible price to pay for that too. Unsurprisingly James had no money of his own but the agent, for a small undisclosed commission, had arranged for James to pay his debts directly out of his wages. The miners were one very short step from slavery; many would be hard pressed to tell the difference. Their camaraderie, sense of purpose and personal achievement was mostly what sustained them, that and the spirits of ancestors who'd walked the same path.

'Ye'll no be wearing they boots down this mine laddie,' said the burly storeman, pointing accusingly at James' boots.

'But they're all I have sir,' James replied apologetically.

'Well, they're no use here laddie, do you want to kill us all? The nails on the soles laddie. . . sparks and gas dinnae mix. I have some old boots o'er here, come and take a look, see if any fit ye.' The storeman ushered James over to a shelf upon which several pairs of second hand boots looked back hopefully at him.

There was a pair on the left that looked just right, they called to him from the shelf, it was without doubt they that chose James, not he them. They fitted fine, in fact they felt fine, better than James imagined someone else's boots could ever feel.

'Aye, a fine choice laddie, a grand pair of boots, they belonged to the late 'Sad Tam' you'll find his name written inside, you can change it for your own later. That'll be five shillings on your company bill.' 'Next!' he shouted, then louder, 'Come along lads I've not all day.'

James was blessed with an easy day, his mentor, an old miner he only ever knew as Danny and who had something of an Irish accent to him, told him to make the most of it as it would be his first and last easy day at the mine. Danny was to show

James the ropes so to speak, where he must go and how he must act, to what work he would be put and the key safety rules he must obey. They both ate that day at the lodging house, which James had noticed often seemed to serve meals for many of the miners even though not actually lodging there.

'Tripe and tatties again James, we get a lot of that. On special days it might be good beef mince, turnips and tatties, that's a lovely dinner, we look forward to that to be sure,' Danny said wiping his sleeve across his mouth, 'I see you've a fine pair of boots James, are they yours?

James looked down at them proudly, then across to Danny, 'Yes, they are now, five bob they cost, I think I'll not be seeing any wages for months at this rate. They have 'Sad Rab' written inside, did you know him?'

'To be sure I did, everybody knew Sad Rab. His real name was Robert, he had no other name we knew of, neither I suspect, did he. He was an orphan and joined the mining as a boy; he had no bad habits, no drinking, smoking or other wild pursuits, he was careful with his money, as you can tell by those fine boots you wear today. He always wanted a family, the family he missed so much. He was a good man and his name belied the kind and warm hearted soul that he was, we all liked him and wished he could fulfil his dreams. . . as we'd like to do with our own too.' Danny continued, 'I can see in your eyes, you want to know if he found his family. Well it wasn't ever to be; Rab was killed in a roof fall about a year ago. That's nothing special by the way, for the mine is full of the souls of accidentally killed miners. Look, you can see the scuff marks down the heels of his, I mean your boots, where they dragged him out. He was a good man and you couldn't walk in a finer man's shoes. He'd be happy for you, to be sure.'

Life was hectic for James for several months as his body and mind slowly became attuned to the strenuous labours of mining work. Mostly he was just labouring at the beck and call of the experienced men. He was stuck on all the worse shifts that older men avoided wherever possible. 'It's the way of it I'm afraid, Richmond,' explained the foreman one day, 'it will change eventually, vacancies will appear for one reason or another and new miners will arrive, then it'll be their turn but until that day you're stuck with the shifts you're given.' The foreman was sympathetic enough but still an authoritatively stern man; he appreciated that James was a likeable and conscientious worker and should do well in the future; James would just have to learn patience.

The seasons and months rushed by with nary a thought from James of going home, he was now far too busy.

He'd soon made good friends with John from London who he'd met on the train. John, though always somehow behind with his debts, couldn't be described as a trouble maker though it frequently sought him out. About a year or more into their service, John persuaded James to go with him and a few others drinking in the nearest town. It didn't suit James really as he was just clearing his debts and had begun to save money for his promised trip home. He thought of his parents and how pleased they'd be with what he had achieved, him standing on his own feet and making his own way in life, yes they'd be proud of him. Not being a drinker by habit the drink went straight to James' head and it wasn't long before John, his so called friend, had talked him into buying drinks for all and sundry. The next day while feeling very much the worse for wear, James was a very remorseful man when he felt in his now empty pockets. He knew that he'd not get home for a good while yet. He must save again. He had a faint recollection of some sort of brawl at the pub but he himself had no marks to show he was involved. At breakfast James saw the evidence of trouble all over his friend's face and hands. John dismissed any questions out of hand, 'Twas nothing, I've been in much worse, they might well be sorry they picked on me, that's all I'm going to say.'

A few days later when John didn't appear for breakfast or lunchtime, James asked if any one had seen him about. It was Mrs McLeod who spoke, 'I think we've seen the last of yon young John, the Polis took him away in the night. Not your local Bobbies either. . . all the way from London they were. They said John wasn't his real name and they'd been looking for him for some time. Just his fate eh, he's obviously been a very naughty boy and now he's been called away to pay for it.'

James felt some sympathy for his taken friend, for no matter what he may have done in the past he'd been a good friend to him, James only knew the good in him, cheeky as he was; Must have been something serious, mind. They never heard any more, it was as though John never was and in any case soon another would take his place. It was simply the way of the world they inhabited.

Months turned into as many years and still James never made it home. Sometimes he feared he'd been away so long that should he return he would find his parents angry with him. The longer he stayed away the more guilt he felt. It almost became easier to mindfully forsake his parents and never think of going home, he felt ashamed that he had abandoned his family so.

James worked hard and saved as much as he could but fate conspired against him to spend it on a journey home. Once it was spent on maintaining the rent on his lodgings after an accident damaged his hands and he could not work for a few weeks. Nobody was allowed to live in a miner's house without being a working miner, widows and their children weren't immune from eviction either, for no profit was ever to be made by such charity. Nobody said life was fair.

Sad Rab's boots eventually wore out and James bought another pair; they were just ordinary boots not like Rab's. He'd thought most often of his parents and home when he wore those second-hand boots, the new boots had no such effect but until his feet had broke them in, they gave him many a blister; so much so he began to wonder which was actually being broken in, those boots or his feet.

Sometimes all James knew was the dark. The dark of night and the dark of the pit blended seamlessly into one, especially in the winter. The pit was relatively warm; sometimes he reckoned it was warmer than his lodgings. Working down the mine was not without its moments of fear for James, though in general he was lucky. However, the accident that damaged his hands brought the occasional nightmare to his sleep.

After an unconnected incident in the same mine, the fear became a reality and he was awake to it, oh so wide awake. They were part of a rescue team to reach miners the other side of a roof fall and the gap they had to squeeze through seemed to James like some evil beast that sought to trap him and grip him underground until he could breathe no more and he turned to bones. James remembered how he had anxiously hesitated and another miner had taken the lead and gone first, making it through the dark, twisted gap to shine his safety lamp back through. The first miner was a bigger man than James and so he knew he shouldn't get stuck – but still frightening none the less. James would ever carry a tinge of guilt for his self presumed cowardice. James had great respect for his mining colleagues, they were a tight knit community and they looked after each other like a strong family. In fact they seemed to have become his family. When asked when he was going home, he always said perhaps this year, but the years rolled on inexorably. Sometimes just before sleep, 'I must go home, I must go home,' he would say to himself, 'I wonder how you are Mother, are you both well?'

In the morning though, it was back to the routine world of work and survival.

**

Now was the year he intended to go, 'I'm definitely going home this year, perhaps in the autumn, yes it's home for me this year,' he told his pals one winter breakfast time.

'You see that you do boy, just you see you do,' Mrs McLeod admonished, 'your mother and father must think you're past dead by now, this year you make sure you go and see them. Time to go home boy.'

'That's telling ye laddie, ye'd better make sure ye go this time,' said one of the old timers, stoutly slapping James' back and raising a black dust that slowly settled on table and porridge alike.

'Will you help me write to my mother, Mrs McLeod? I'll go home to see them this year. I'll let them know I'm coming,' exclaimed a newly excited James. It would seem that having made a firm decision, the weight that had played on his mind was lifted, he felt good about his choice, very good.

'That I will, James. Remind me later and we'll put pen to paper for your mother,' replied Mrs McLeod, who had taken a liking to this worthy young lad over the years he'd stayed at her lodgings.

A new recruit to join the mining village, poor unfortunate soul, was to bring with him the inevitable seed of disaster, a terrible disease of the times. It wasn't long before the few contacts he had made went down with a debilitating sickness. Typhus, rumour said it was; however, the mine was kept open and the miners kept working, they had targets to meet and their wages depended upon reaching them. After about a week, James also began to feel unwell himself and took to his bed, well, to be fair he didn't take to it but one morning he just couldn't find the strength to get out of it. He was to weaken rapidly and within a few days was reduced to a very sorry state indeed. Mrs McLeod had a word with the visiting doctor; a well liked fair and honest woman, she was on good terms with all. The doctor examined James and concluded that it was probably typhus he had, chances were, him being a strong young man, he would recover.

'He may well pull through on his own Helen,' he spoke quietly at the doorway, 'I'll leave you some Laudanum for him, it will ease any pains, I'll call by tomorrow. I would keep it quiet a while, for I know the mine owners want any sick miners unable to work to be gone. We'll see how he is tomorrow, must be away now, God bless you for your kind heart Helen.'

'You too Doctor - you too,' she said clasping the small bottle in both hands. 'Thank you Doctor - thank you.'

It was early evening before the doctor returned the next day; James was deteriorating and drifting in and out of a delirium, whether from the Laudanum or the fever we'll never know. He could no longer see but could hear occasional voices, sometimes he felt there was a woman's presence, his mother came to mind and in that mind he was going home. In his mind he was at the little cottage door calling for his mother.

'Sorry, Helen, nothing more I can do, the company won't pay for his treatment and want him away. I have persuaded them in their own interest to arrange transport to the isolation hospital at Browick Glen, two stops down the track. They will tend to his needs there. Does he have family?' the Doctor's voice was caring and solemn.

'Oh dear, yes,' she was jolted by a guilty memory. 'We were supposed to write a letter to his mother one time, I clean forgot, only James knew the address mind, so I'll not be able to write for him. Oh my goodness and he was going home this year too. They'll never know,' she said mournfully.

'You've done your best Helen, nothing more you can do now, it's almost over. I'll make arrangements for the morrow. You must get some rest too,' and with that he turned and left for home.

For James what was left of life, if you could call it such, was quite weird and wonderful, possibly the drugs the doctor had so generously left or perhaps the delirium caused by the fever. Sometimes he thought he heard voices, sometimes he thought he was flying and could see himself from above; sometimes he fleetingly saw people, not always clearly and afterwards could not recall who they were. If indeed he ever did know them. It was time he went home. In fact he knew he was going home, he felt the cold outside air on his face and smelled the coal smoke and steam of the locomotive; he heard the mesmerising clickety clack of iron wheels on the familiar iron track. In his own mind, the journey home had begun and how so very much he looked forward to seeing his mother and father. James smiled peacefully as he felt again like he was floating on air, 'so much easier than that awful journey away from home up to Scotland,' he thought, 'so much easier.' At this point in time he was being stretchered from the station at Browick Glen to the isolation hospital's wagon.

'Never seen one in such a bad state with a smile on their face before,' uttered the orderly to his companion.

'Nor I,' came the reply, 'from the doctor's note we'll be as well to forget the hospital and take him straight to the graveyard.' They both smiled the smiles of men with tough jobs to do but who countered their pain with a humour that few on the outside would ever understand.

James felt the floating sensation again as he was lifted to the wagon, then the weight of blankets to keep him warm.

To James the steady rocking motion of the wagon, the clip clop of horse's hooves and the crunch of iron rimmed wheels on gravel were just a short and happy carriage ride to the old farm and home.

Meanwhile down south, at the farm labourer's little cob and thatch cottage, darkness was to arrive unexpectedly early that evening. Henry lit the oil lamp and thoughtfully put the last of their coal on the fire. Martha Richmond stared at the rain-dropped darkness of the small window pane and for one wild moment she imagined she had seen a gaunt unshaven face beckoning her. It made her suddenly think of James, the beloved son she had prayed for every night since he'd gone away and it made her wonder out loud.

'I just know he'll come home Henry, a mother knows these things you know. . . he will come home, something tells me he'll be home,' she spoke softly with a certain air of prophecy in her voice.

'No use you staring out that window any more Martha, I fear we will not see him again, God bless him. For all we know he could be dead. If he weren't we'd surely have heard some news from him by now,' said a more stoical Henry, doing what was his considered level best to comfort his grieving wife.

Henry closed the wooden shutters to the other world beyond the glass and adjusted the oil lamp flame. They both sat close by to their dwindling fire, 'Not much coal left dear,' said Henry, as wind blown rain tapped feverishly like an impatient but unheard visitor on their little cottage window and a dispossessed wind howled a timely lament under their door.

Footnote:- The end; for us as much as it was for them.

While James' spirit had pleaded to his mother through the rain pattered window, the wagon arrived at the isolation Hospital doors and his body succumbed to the inevitable. As much as his body would never return to the little farm cottage his spirit would never return to his body, for now his spirit had no home. Even to this day when the dark and wind blown rain is at hand he still taps on the window of the little cottage, notwithstanding it has now stood empty for some eighty years or more.

**

'Destiny comes not through chance but by choice.
You are your own destiny.'

THE OUIJA BOARD – HANNAH'S TALE.

It was coming to the end of another pleasant lunch time in the local council office canteen, Dr Joseph Dewar placed his near empty cup quietly on the saucer and looked across at his old friend Bob Rathbone; they'd been close friends since studying history together at Cambridge many years before. Glancing about him to see who might be in earshot, Dr Dewar confided, 'There you have it then Bob, it's an old basement still in a structurally safe condition, probably covered over since the Blitz, the developers will be filling it in very shortly but as you know we are obliged to give it the archaeological once over before they can continue. Well, we did and we've finished with it. I carried out the investigation myself and if I can feel the energy down there then sure as hell you will too. It would make a terrific place for a séance and as long as you can keep hush-hush about it, I can provide you with access this weekend. Sunday is best - we don't want the politically correct and health and safety mob snooping around. The nature of your interests doesn't exactly enamour you to the establishment.'

Bob smiled the smile of the eternally grateful, 'Joe, that would be brilliant, truly terrific, I have some new people interested in the spiritual arts, this is an opportunity sent from heaven. I'll make arrangements for us to meet up at the venue on Sunday, say about ten in the morning?' Dr Dewar simply nodded his head in agreement.

The scene for the grand séance was now set. Bob Rathbone, professional psychic and erstwhile pursuer of all things strange and supernatural was soon back in his home and busy with the telephone, organising participants and swearing them to the most binding of secrecy. They were all told where and when they should meet and that Bob was especially intending to use the Ouija board. Access would already have been left open for them on the Sunday morning by his friend Dr Dewar. They knew it was going to be a special event for they could sense the excitement in Bob's voice - plus it was all hush-hush, a really secret meeting, one to get the blood itself tingling. No one would ever know what was going on underground that day; it would be a case of out of sight, out of mind.

Sunday came apace.

Before the others arrived, Hannah, her cold and fear already overcome, was waiting on the bottom brick steps of the basement. It seemed like she had waited an eternity and she had long wondered if any one was ever coming. Then she heard them arrive, she heard their eager voices with offers of help; help to carry Bob's folding chairs and little card table, always so useful for such events. The dim light in the basement darkened deeper as the little group of spirit seekers blotted out the light of day at the basement entrance and very carefully filed down the shadowy brick steps. Politely as was ever her way, Hannah stood and moved carefully to one side.

Soon, the candle lit table was surrounded by six occupied chairs.

'Okay, good, we're all here, glad you could make it. I hope you've all kept your promise of secrecy. We are some of a very few privileged people to be in this room since the blitz of some seventy years ago. Please make yourself as comfortable as possible; we don't want to fidget about once we start. Those of you who are new to this just relax and follow along with open minds. I don't anticipate that we will be confined here in the darkness for too long, perhaps a couple of hours at most,' explained Bob in his calm almost hypnotic voice, then with a grand flourish he took out his much loved antique Ouija board and placed it reverently on the dark green baize of the table. There was a veritable quiver of excitement; a truly tangible presence in the air. Next Bob took the planchette or pointer from his pocket; it was wrapped in a piece of well worn black velvet. 'Now this,' Bob continued, 'is really something special, this heart shaped planchette is made from wood I salvaged from Bethany Street Church after it burned down the other year. It's the first time I've used it in the presence of others; I've a good feeling all should go well today and we will soon contact any spirits present.'

Hannah was fascinated by it all, she had a strange feeling that this event was always meant to be, a sort of destiny; she felt like it was a chance to expurgate her demons and in some way perhaps find the spiritual freedom she had past been denied. For Hannah, this Ouija board signified a prospect of almost breathtaking proportions. It was an invitation she could not turn down.

While everyone else sat quietly, their minds filled with anticipation, excitement and not a little trepidation too, Bob's soft voice reached out to the group and into the encompassing darkness. 'There are a few things I'd like to tell the new people before we start. If we do contact spirits, then it is often said that they are usually spirits of a lower plane. Spirits confused about how to move on, murders, suicides and the like, when the victim's spirit was never given time to accept and adapt. At body death such a spirit may create an emotional bond with their immediate surroundings, perhaps like this basement. It is a little like the imprinting of new-borns on the first animal they contact in their new surroundings. There are many who say that what we do is all fake, you need to be aware of this scepticism and be extra careful about what you share with others. They will not understand. You must make up your own mind based on experience. Seriously now; what we are about to do is open a doorway to abnormal dimensions. The board itself cannot harm you, however, your own mind may. This is true in any walk of life but when it exposes your innate centre to possibly quite frightening and inexplicable experiences it can haunt you for the rest of your life.'

The situation in the basement became serious and to more than one of them it seemed a little colder than when they first came in; a cool breeze had sprung up that had touched their faces like passing cobwebs. Bob took a small piece of dried sage and lit it from one of the candles. As his hand fanned the smouldering ember's perfumed smoke around the table, he asked that the spirits allow this place to be clean and good.

If it didn't affect any spirits, it certainly gave great comfort to the waiting group.

'Now please,' said Bob in a firm and positive tone, 'all those in the group who wish to join in, place your finger on the planchette, otherwise just remain still and calm and watch. Those joining in may ask their own simple questions, keeping them positive and not expecting any long answers.'

Just four of the group chose to place their fingers on the board's heart shaped pointer.

Bob spoke first, 'We come with truly compassionate hearts seeking to contact the spirit world. . . is there anyone here?'

After a brief pause, the pointer seemed to move all of its own accord to 'yes.' Somebody in the group gasped; the following all pervading grave like silence filled only with the pounding of their own heartbeats.

Hannah sat quietly just observing, absolutely calm, simply spellbound by the whole event unfolding before her; She began to imagine that the séance was especially for her, and her alone.

Next, a young man called Finley nervously asked, 'Was this your home?'

He was disappointed when the pointer did not move but Bob intervened and encouraged Finley again, 'It's not moved Finley because the spirit is repeating the 'yes,' well done.'

'Are you a man?' asked Betty, a sixty something stalwart of the psychic group. The pointer moved leisurely but surely to 'no.'

Finley couldn't wait to ask again, 'What's your name please?'

It took some time to spell it out as the pointer moved purposely but slowly to the letters, as if the spirit was old, frail or perhaps just thoughtful. . . 'H' 'A' 'N.'. . 'N' 'A' 'H.'. .

Nobody spoke a word and the silence took on a perceptibly eerie quality.

Hannah thought deeply and privately to herself, 'Why, that's my name, how amazing, what a strange coincidence. I wonder what will happen next?'

Bob took over, 'Hannah, thank you for showing we are not alone down here, we are indebted for your contact. May I ask when you passed to spirit?'

'1' '9' '4' '2' came the clear response.

'That's a long time ago Hannah; were you affected by the war that was happening at that time?'

The pointer moved much more rapidly and instantly to 'yes.'

Bob picked up on the sense of agitation and angst that his question had caused but he continued cautiously, asking several questions that related to Hannah's life during the Second World War on the home front. The spirit seemed desperate to answer, almost seeming to be impatiently waiting, waiting for the next question to come, just waiting; forever waiting.

The candles were half-burned down by now and Bob was feeling hungry and suspected the others may be too, he had also noticed a couple in the group shivering with cold on occasions, 'Okay, group, it is time we left Hannah in peace, we will once again thank her spirit for being with us, we will clean the board again with burning sage and we will meet at my house Tuesday evening to discuss our experiences. Thank you all, thank you Hannah and goodbye.'

With that said and done, the group picked up their chairs and climbed the brick steps, once again dimming the basement to obscurity as they themselves breathed fresh air and escaped the darkness they left behind.

Monday saw the ever impatient developer's bulldozers and diggers move in to do what they do best, flatten things. The basement was filled in and levelled over. Soon concrete sealed the darkness forever and work began on the new council car park.

Accordingly, during Tuesday lunchtime Bob met again with his friend Dr Dewar, senior county archaeologist, at the council office canteen.

As Bob smiled the smile of the eternally grateful, he confided, 'Terrific visit Joe, so good of you to think of me, can't thank you enough, amazing place and atmosphere. We managed to reach a spirit called Hannah, such a pretty evocative name, more unusual these days, I've not heard it spoken in a long while. Anyway it would seem that she lived at that address and died in 1942, something to do with the war. All six of us had a wonderful time, regulars like Finley and Betty told me it was one of the best ever and it was a first-rate introduction to the three newcomers, Rowena, Mike and Vanessa, absolutely superb it was.'

Dr Joseph Dewar leaned forward and slid a brown paper file across the table, 'Bob,' he said in half whisper, 'I did the archaeological investigation myself as you may recall me saying, I neglected to tell you that we actually recovered unidentified skeletal remains from the premises.'

The file cover read:

Archaeology Dept
Ref 3021,
Basement
Old Calcutta Road Development

Bob expectantly opened the file and glanced at a few drawings, notes and photographs which he quickly recognised as 'Hannah's' basement. One photo specifically caught his eye, the location of the skeleton. . . slumped about the bottom two steps of the brick stairs.

Dr Dewar continued his analytical revelation, 'An elderly female, height about five feet four, probably in her early to mid eighties, some signs of rickets and arthritis but otherwise no trauma. It is my considered opinion that she lived alone and was trapped and left in the basement following an officially recorded air raid on that area in, as you so rightly said, 1942. I tried the records office to confirm occupancy during that period but no relevant documents have survived intact. I think the poor soul starved to death or possibly asphyxiated while trapped in the basement. It must have seemed one terrifying time without end to her. Chances are that no one knew she was there and the basement was well hidden with rubble, which is why it has only come to light recently with the building works going on. From our available evidence, there was no way I could formally identify the remains.'

Bob Rathbone, professional psychic and erstwhile pursuer of all things strange and supernatural, reflected with a new understanding upon events, sensitively he shut the file and slid it back across the table, nodding sympathetically.

Dr Joseph Dewar, archaeologist and forensic scientist, took a pen from his inside jacket pocket and deftly wrote on the file cover:

'HANNAH'S BASEMENT - FILE CLOSED.'

**

I can tell you no more, for I too am sworn to secrecy, and perhaps I have said too much already. . .

**

'If you don't keep quiet, you will never hear the echo.'

THE TORRINGTON ROAD GIBBET.

It was Doreen's first time in Bideford, she'd come to visit her old pen pal Pamela, who lived in a little terraced cottage on the hill beyond the police station. They first met through a little known spiritual organisation, an ancient collective for those with interests in 'the other world.'

It was early September and a pleasant evening about an hour before sunset when the two friends took a stroll by the riverbank and out along the Torrington road.

'What a strange place this is, and, if I didn't know better, I'd be frightened,' said Doreen.

'Well Dor, you're the one to know what's strange, what with your spirit dealings and all that. You've certainly always impressed me, I just don't know how you do it, I really don't,' replied Pam, still wondering just what was so strange.

'Fancy you still having one of those awful things here,' continued Doreen, pointing an accusing finger just down the road from the junction, 'there, look, on the left of the road.'

'I can't see anything Dor,' said Pam peering over the top of her glasses and scouring the rising river mists for what strange thing could be out there.

Doreen didn't pause for breath, 'Well, I'll go to the foot of our stairs if it isn't a gibbet of all things; awful things they were too. . . and something tells me this one has a story to tell. Come on, let's go closer.' Pam was happy enough to go along with this suggestion, after all it was still close to town, it was still light and Doreen was obviously on a mission; Doreen could 'see' many a thing that ordinary folk could not.

'Pam. . . did once a highwayman ply his evil trade along this road?' inquired Doreen.

'Never heard of one Dor, not that I know of anyway,' she replied slowly shaking her head in thought, then she went quiet as Doreen appeared to be listening to someone else.

'Is there anybody there?' Doreen asked calmly, 'Please come closer. What is it you want?'

Though it was a calm and warm evening, Pam felt a cold breeze by her ankles and something soft brushed her face; she could hear nothing but Doreen's murmured conversation and the light rumble of traffic crossing the medieval long bridge in the distance. After twenty minutes or so, Doreen was back in the present. Turning towards town she said, 'Come on Pamela, back to your house, and I'll tell you all. There's work for us to do here!'

They entered the house by the back door, 'Go on. . . what did you find out, Dor?'

'Kettle on first Pam, then, pen and paper and we'll sit at the kitchen table. There is much to tell. . .'

**

'His name was Tom, though not sure how old he was, he thinks he was an orphan. He was probably about twenty five years of age, a swarthy young man, scruffy and unkempt, with dark straggly hair. Locals called him 'Black Tom.' He'd been a runaway apprentice and could neither read nor write, something that no doubt contributed to his demise. He lived almost wild, surviving hand to mouth, begging from travellers on the Torrington road. Tom was befriended by the somewhat astute and outwardly benevolent landlord of an Inn, an Inn of ill repute some few miles between the two towns. Tom could often get a meal there for running errands or cleaning out the stables;

sometimes he would sleep in them, despite the Inn being drenched in an apparent evil best avoided. A blurry image came to me as he described the Inn, close by the river it was, a low, cob built building with a thatched roof, next to it leaned similarly built stables, there was a small carriage outside and about four or five horses, fine looking animals, not cart horses. Grey smoke came from a single chimney in the middle of the roof. I caught a glimpse of armed men running about, then the vision vanished into blackness and I found myself with Tom again, listening to his tale of woe. The Landlord was a powerfully built charismatic man called Rufus Hench, though that may not have been his real name.'

Pamela nodded an acknowledgement of the name and promptly made some notes.

Doreen continued, 'Rufus was very popular with travellers, always plying them generously with drink and meat and befriending them. In those far away days, many a traveller would fall prey to some devious nearby highwayman and it wasn't unknown for a lone traveller never to finish their journey. The local magistrate and squire would often meet at the Inn to discuss their plans to catch this vicious local footpad.

Poor Tom still can't understand why it was him they beat, dragged away, tried and hanged. Rufus Hench had promised Tom he would put in a good word for him at the trial but in the event did not turn up and in consequence Tom stood alone, illiterate and defenceless against his accusers. Poor Tom's body was displayed on the gibbet we saw, as a severe warning to any would be thieves that came that way. After the hanging, the robberies stopped.'

Pamela finished making her notes and with an air of excitement proclaimed, 'Tomorrow Doreen, we'll go to our town library and see what we can dig up, I know the lady in there, I'll phone first so she can help us better.'

**

Later the next day, they climbed the few steps that entered the town library, 'Hi Pam. . . and you must be Doreen, Pam's friend, welcome,' said Rosey the reference librarian, 'after your phone call I had a good search of our archives. Not such good news I'm afraid, come on through to the back office and I'll show you what we have.'

They gathered around the desk upon which various documents, old and new were scattered.

'Right,' said Rosey, 'the bad news; no record or even vague inference anywhere to an Inn on that road, no highwayman, no 'Black Tom' and no gibbet either. The good news is we have a lot on Rufus Hench. He was a very rich man who apparently came from London and commissioned a fine house to be built on the quay. According to the records he came to the town just before the civil war. He appears to have been very popular and generous and soon became not only Mayor but also Customs and Excise Officer, in which distinguished capacity he served for fourteen years until he emigrated taking his wealth with him; after that he seems to have disappeared completely from public life. Unfortunately there are very few records that survived from before Mayor Hench's time due to an accidental fire only a few months after he was elected. Only the fire and any subsequent history remain on record. Sorry about that, perhaps your Tom the highwayman did exist, but now I'm afraid no one will ever know the truth.'

'I suspect in our hearts we already knew the answer Pam,' empathized Doreen as the pair left the library to walk soulfully up the High Street.

Perhaps one quiet day, if you're out along the Torrington Road and the mists are rising from the river you too might hear Black Tom's cry for justice. . .

**

'And as a single leaf turns not yellow
but with the silent knowledge of the whole tree,
So the wrong-doer cannot do wrong
without the hidden will of you all.'

Gibran (The Prophet)

Tales that reach out to the soul

Written in a slightly different style than many others in this series of short tales, these stories may at times touch on a gentle humour, yet never stray from the seriousness of an intended message.

NO FREE LUNCH TOMORROW.
(Why are we so surprised when the 'bill' arrives?)

Allegedly, originating from a trusted source which wishes to remain anonymous for fear of reprisals, this could all well be true. I can say no more on the matter except here is the story.

There was once a very wealthy but mean farmer, Moriarty Crippin, Esquire by name. As well as several other of God's creatures within the grip of his tender mercies, he farmed chickens.

His extensive and grand 16th century farm, much of it born from land grabbing through the Inclosure Acts of England, was separated by a clear running, gravel bedded shallow stream from his nearest neighbour's quaint but dilapidated thatched cottage.

In the said cottage lived a little old widow lady, Florence Darling by name, who in her dotage tried her best to grow a few vegetables of her own and who also kept a couple of chickens. Her hens were getting long in the tooth, metaphorically so to speak, but she thought the world of all living creatures and her hens were guaranteed to see a happy old age, eggs or not. Florence's garden was a haven for wildlife, Robins and Blackbirds nested in the overgrown hedgerow and Hedgehogs lived under it, waiting for their night time beetle, slug and snail patrol in the garden. The kind old lady didn't mind the moles visiting either. . . it was a garden of tranquil energy.

Unfortunately and despite the fine sunny weather, her hens were temporarily off lay (she hoped that such was the case anyway) and she was short of eggs for her baking day. As it happened she spotted her neighbour admiring her garden from across the stream and went out to speak with him, 'Oh, good morning Mr Crippin, how are you this fine morning?'

Moriarty Crippin Esq was briefly shaken out of his thoughts on what a God forsaken mess that old woman had made of a piece of land that had somehow errantly slipped through his ancestor's needy grasp. He'd been staring with livid intent upon the brambles and nettles that appeared to be queuing up on the far bank, just itching to cross over into his own neat but sterile grasslands, 'Oh, yes, good morning to you too Darling.' He only ever addressed people by their surname; it was a question of status, his, to be precise. In his own, venerable opinion the peasant class must ever be sure of their place in the pecking order.

Dear old Florence smiled and continued, 'It's my weekly baking day today Mr Crippin and I'm a little short of eggs, I wonder if you can spare a few. Just this once of course.'

Moriarty Crippin Esq was incredulous and almost incandescent with affronted rage but he hid it well; a skill he'd learned from a close but closet politician friend. He couldn't give a fig if this little old tramp-like woman was short of eggs, why didn't she buy her groceries on line like his housekeeper did - stupid woman. Perhaps when she finally got around to dying, he'd get that piece of land at last, her having no children as far as he knew. Weed killer and bulldozers came to mind, his mind, for a start.

In more ways than one, he looked down on her from the elevated stream bank of his farm. Adjusting the lapels of his Tweed jacket with his thumbs, 'Eggs aren't free you know, Darling, they don't grow on trees. You'll have to pay and I'm not sure we have eggs to spare in any case,' he lectured, his voice a strange cross between a pontificating, vilifying manner and someone whose favourite dog was just dying.

He knew full well that the old widow lady had no means to pay the sort of prices he demanded for free range eggs from vaccinated chickens (he'd no idea what against but he was told he could offset the entire cost against tax, so he'd had them done.)

Unfortunately for Mrs Darling she had badly misread the nature of Moriarty Crippin Esq, thinking that he was a kindly nature lover akin to herself. 'At least I'll have one egg off you today,' she smiled naively, 'just like most days.'

'Oh, and how is that then, Darling,' retorted the sneakily mean and rapidly becoming tetchy Moriarty. (If I may be so bold to call him that.)

'Every day, well, nearly every day, one of your hens crosses the stream, over there by the shallows,' she said, pointing with her arthritic left hand, 'and after wandering in my garden with the others, she lays an egg in the hen house nest box. Oh, she is a little beauty, such a good nature, light brown fluffy thing she is; Don't you worry about the eggs if you can't help Mr Crippin, not to worry,' smiled Florence with her hands crossed and resting on her apron clad tummy.

Next day a smiling Moriarty Crippin Esq called Florence to the stream. She shuffled over as quickly as she could, wiping her hands on a tea towel as she went, suspecting that her kindly neighbour had found her some eggs after all.

'I just thought you should know that there will be no more free eggs. . . not from that hen anyway,' he said with coroner-like certainty. He washed some blood off the spade in the stream and turned to replace it in his garden shed. Crippin then stomped his lordly green gumboots in the direction of his manor.

Just as the little hen had so often freely done in life, her blood meandered down the stream followed by a single tear from Florence. Florence stood quietly and motionless, each hand holding the other for comfort, until the stream ran clear again and all seemed as it was before. Of course it never could be. No free lunch tomorrow.

Someone must always pay; there is no free lunch in life.

**

'The apple tree never discriminates.
Anyone can pick an apple.'

NOBLE NOIRE MORTE AND HIS INTREPID TREK THROUGH LIFE.

The tragic story of a kindly rat that one day travelled too far from home.

It had been a long, troubled and several months' journey on which our young Noire Morte had embarked from his home town of Bubonika; a charming little forest village that snuggled deep in the east of Europe. Travelling mostly by night and often stowing away on any transport he could find that was run by the feared two legged giants. Yet the fishing boat he'd taken from France had been in some small way a blessed bonus to him, he'd had a chance to rest and to feed well on the debris of cheese and salami at the crew's table. The crew having joined in spirit the already sleeping red wine they had so liberally quaffed, with increasingly blurred vision and distorted cries of 'Salut,' 'Shalut,' 'Salutsh.'

He ate well and he slept well in the sea air. By day and by night he'd roamed the fish stained decks as he'd pleased, almost as if he were the Captain himself. Ah, what times he'd had aboard La Belle Josephine; (a totally unsuitable name for such a floating wreck). Noire remembered thinking at the time that it was strange that other rats weren't already living on board, he'd chuckled to himself as he renamed her the 'Not Tonight Josephine.' . .'Or any night come to think of it!' The thought alone smirkled his face and his charming little rodent chuckle joined in with the mocking laugh of the gulls.

Customs at the British port was easier than he ever could have imagined, as he walked though the unmanned gates he read a sign:

Declare all contraband to the Authorities;
If guilty make yourself known to an officer.

Underneath some one had written in felt tip:

If you can find one!

Next to this sign he saw a poster calling all three Union members to a meeting about some further proposed right-wing draconian redundancies in the service: guest speaker, Karl 'Trotsky' Scraghill; followed by a fish supper and a pint in the Dog and Bloater. And yet one more sign to read before he finally tired of reading them,

'VACANCIES: urgently wanted for customs services.
Management Consultants (3)
Public Relations and Media Control (3 full time)
(2 part time or job share)
Car Parking Infringement Officer (Ideal candidate needs
psychopathic tendencies or to have served time in Parkhurst or
Barlinney). Good rates of pay and annual bonus.
No experience necessary. No applications entertained
from existing or past customs staff

Noire made his thoughtful way westwards, he was a superbly skilled navigator and, unlike the giants, he needed no GPS, maps nor the internet AA for directions. Noire was just a natural genius; the stars, the Sun, the Earth's magnetic field, the only tools he needed, those, endurance and courage. He worked hard, never letting up on his long held dream, to visit his now dying grandmother on the south west coast. He often foraged for his own food in the wild and on occasions did the giants a favour by cleaning up discarded burger and pizza debris from night time pavements of small towns he had to traverse. 'What awful, dirty people these giants are,' he thought. 'Why they dislike us so I'll never understand. Are we not all God's creatures? What do we do that destroys our lovely Earth? Nothing. We are the true eco warriors.'

Day by day, night by night Noire trudged on, the weeks went by as the miles accumulated behind him. Few would think that those little legs could take him so far but they didn't know the heart and mind that drove them on, onwards and Atlantic bound to see his dying kin.

As he came closer to the roar of sea on rocks and the rumble of rounded stones pulled out to sea by the undertow, he knew he was close but also that he must rest a while and gain his strength before visiting dear old Granny Noirette. He was in luck, for there, in the litter-strewn country lane, discarded from a passing tourist's car was an advert for bed and breakfast, not more than a couple of miles from where he stood nor far from where he was going. 'Perfect,' he thought. 'Perfect. . . and they speak multiple languages there too. . . and animals were welcome.' Oh, music to his ears it was as he read it out loud to himself, how wonderful it will be. He folded the advert neatly and took it with him to dispose of properly.

When he arrived at the B&B he took in the five bar gate, the freshly mown lawns and some brown chickens next door, then he walked fearlessly past a big dog laying out on the concrete yard. 'Morning fatty,' he joked cheekily, assuming he was a fellow guest. 'Fatty's' head slumped back to the floor and his eyes closed as he dreamt on of a B&B in Canada and Moose dinners and snow and things.

Noire went round the back of the big white house and was pleasantly surprised to see other guests were still at breakfast, there were obviously a number of birds staying there. . . but what was among them? None other than a close cousin of his in fancy dress. Yes, it was Nutty Scurridae, dressed up in a squirrel costume.

'Nuts, Nuts, is that you old boy?' he shouted, frightening many of the guests away from their seed and fruit feast.

'Ooarh, 'tis I, 'tis I, how are ee be old Noire?' 'Nuts' showed Noire some comfy accommodation along the back hedge.

'Is it safe here Nuts?' enquired a tired but careful Noire.

'Oh yes, indeed it be. Free food laid on every day and fresh it be too. I'm very popular here, well liked by the lady giant who's a bit of a softy, you'll like her. The bloke giant, well, a bit odd but good enough as it's him that feeds us our breakfasts.'

A reassured Noire dropped his guard and stayed for a very peaceful and pleasant few days; his fur soon began to take on a renewed sheen and his footpads no longer pained him to walk. Then Noire decided it was time to leave; he was now re-freshed and strong enough to move on to visit his dear old Granny. 'Right, one more farewell breakfast with cousin Nuts and the other lovely guests then I'll be on my way,' he yawned to himself as he finished his usual early morning yoga stretches and shamanic meditations. Everyone was already there eating when he arrived at the al fresco tables and as he tucked in to some sunflower seed that appeared to have been left out in the open in a little heap just for him, he uttered a sacred shamanic prayer for the kindly giants of the big white house.

He was never to hear the shot echo across the valley; his con-fused mind briefly sensed his lifeless body slumping to the cold, now heartless, ground. The gun went back in the giant's cupboard and noble Noire's body was dragged off to the bin. Meanwhile Nuts just kept on eating the bird food. He re-flected, 'This grey costume the family had gotten from the USA was worth its weight in gold.'

As the lights grew dim for Granny Noirette she thought for an instant she saw the figure of her brave young grandson in the doorway. 'Is that you dear? Is that you Noire, my beloved?' There was only a long but poignant silence in reply, and the lights were slowly dimmed forever.

Such was the journey of the young and noble Noire Morte of Bubonika.

Footnote; the villagers of Bubonika started saving so that they could run annual visits to the big white house where in large invited crowds from all over Europe they would hold memorial serv-ices. . . but next time, they would be ready.

**

'Do not look where you fell, but where you slipped.'

RODERICK THE GREEK

The tail of a Greek rat; gymnast,
philosopher and entrepreneur.

It was not so long ago on a beautiful Island in the Ionian Sea, made famous by a film called 'Bo Bo the Gerbil's Violin,' lived the hero of our story, Roderick the rat.

The home of Roderick's parents was a humble affair at the head of a wooded valley looking down to the sea. They struggled to bring up Roderick as their homeland was torn up by an English building site. None the less they taught him well regarding the value of discretion, concealment and the great secrets that even I cannot tell you. A large man, a giant, had moved into the almost complete building at the same time as Roderick's parents told him it was time to go and fend for himself.

The young Roderick would spend hours at night checking over the progress of the construction site, often finding the odd crisp, crumb or piece of tomato, 'Oh, how thoughtful of him ,' thought Roderick. Roderick thought so highly of the giant that he would sometimes watch him from the undergrowth even in daylight, never minding the hunting buzzards patrolling the clear blue sky.

'Oh, how alike are we,' thought Roderick. 'We both love building, we enjoy the same food and we both spend time meditating. Oh, how wonderful it is to be neighbours with such a fine being.'

The giant built a great temple of a BBQ area, as big, if not bigger than many a Greek bungalow that Roderick had visited with relatives in his childhood. Roderick knew all about BBQs, they were built to honour the Great Rat God, and the living small furry ones that served on earth. Giants would celebrate; drinking and chanting into the night then leave offerings to the little furry ones before retiring for the night.

Roderick loved building and soon was obsessed with being

near his hero giant and he started to build too; a wonderful six room apartment in the woodpile behind the BBQ.

'Ah,' thought Roderick, 'now my Giant friend will never be alone, how wonderful.'

Twice a year, June and September, there would be a great meeting of worshippers from the Giant clan, their special celebrations involved lots of eating, drinking and cavorting as well as the usual chanting and singing. The food left out for Roderick was the very best and in such quantity that his now growing family were well fed and happy. Sometimes Roderick would invite special guests to stay overnight and enjoy the ritual and festivities.

Occasionally Roderick's excitement would get the better of him and he would try to join the Giants, despite this being against the repeated childhood warnings of his loving parents. Sometimes he'd hide behind the outdoor fridge, just so he could be near. Sometimes the visiting worshippers would spot him and this would escalate their festivities into frenzy, and wonders of all wonders they would play his favourite game. . . Hide and seek. If the giants became too disrespectfully boisterous Roderick would show off with some Olympic wall climbing and hundred metres scurry. Oh, such great days, the best of accommodation, warm dry, plenty of food and water but best of all, good company. Oh, such good days, all was well with the world and everyone was happy.

Roderick was in paradise, but he knew he still had far to go on his path to enlightenment. When he was younger he was a bit head strong and was no stranger to the odd fight. Now he'd found a better way to live: a way of peace.

Roderick enjoyed many visitors, many came just to revel in the plush secure surroundings but some would come for therapy, for Roderick was a mystic healer in the rat world. He also taught classes in his old fighting art of Ro Den Do, first brought to the island by a stowaway Japanese rat.

Then one day the Giant was gone. Oh how lonely it was without him but Roderick knew what he must do, he must guard the buildings against intruders and set up a vigil and pray for the Giant's safe return. Roderick had been left in charge of all he could see; what responsibility, what an honour.

Joy of all joys, after some months away and having missed the birth and christening at the local Church of Roderick's latest children the Giant was back.

Roderick was a bit of a psychic too, but was troubled by a dream he had that the Giant would one day turn on his old friend. The nightmares came often but in his waking hours Roderick shrugged them off as delusion, making up all sorts of excuses to explain them away. Too much cheese before sleep . . . watched a horror film about life on the Serengeti through the Giant's window, etc. Any excuse to hide his inner fears.

As it was he had problems enough, his family seemed to be suffering from a virulent disease, he'd heard of it in other parts of the island where the English lived, it was often fatal. His family were dying around him; all his skills were of no avail.

Then, one day Roderick found a special gift left out for him by the giant. 'Oh, how kind. It must be some medicine to help us,' thought Roderick.

Two days later Roderick staggered back to his parent's old home to see his father. In despair he called out for him. How could he know they were already dead?

Meanwhile, as the giant sat down for tea and tiffin in his comfy chair, the Buddha wiped a tear from his eye knowing that his good friend and disciple Roderick was not going to make Nirvana in this life time. 'Ah, old friend,' said the Buddha through the great void, 'needs must when the time is right your spirit will take another form on Earth and you may complete your journey.'

Roderick was to gasp his last painful breath not knowing the secret of reincarnation this time. As he died Roderick blessed his friend the Giant for his shared companionship and shared goals and hoped they would all meet up again in Nirvana, the mythical home of the great rats, and then Roderick could re-turn in full the hospitality to his life long friend, the Giant.

**

'A wise man hears one word but understands two.'

MEDITATION

Was it only a dream?

Outside, a lone honey bee foraged amongst the damp and fading blue Corn Flowers, and an unusually cool wind for the time of year waved the young, burgundy fronds of the Mimosa tree with an invisible hand. Meanwhile indoors, with his arms resting heavily on the old pine kitchen table, he was contemplating on how summer was more like autumn this year. Steam rose from a mug of herbal tea as if it could compete with the playful smoke of burning incense, the little grey wisps of flying dragon smoke, playing all the way to the high ceiling. Scribbled notes on scraps of paper were strewn confusedly on the old table; chaotic as were his thoughts.

As his mind quietened, he drifted off gently into a day dream and soon, sitting before him, were two old people. The woman had the semblance of being English of around the 15th Century and the man seemed of Oriental origin of no known century, though by his clothes he'd led a frugal life. When they spoke, though the dreamer knew not their language, his dream allowed him to intuitively understand what they were saying. The old lady calmly adjusted her shawl and gently placed her hands loosely clasped together on the table, 'We understand that you desire to meditate; what is it that you wish to know?'

At last the dreamer had been sent the help for which he'd hoped for so many years, someone to guide him; 'I don't know; how can I know the unknown, I don't know how or what to look for, yet I know I must look.'

'Good, that's good,' said the old man. 'You're making progress just by realising that there is something there to understand; something out there; something 'beyond,' something to 'believe.''

Once again the old lady's calm voice commanded attention, 'On your journey, though you must search, yet search not too hard, nor try too hard. You cannot 'make' it happen. But do not despair, for you can create the circumstances in which it is possible that it can happen. When it does, neither time nor space will exist for you, you will neither know how long or how far was your journey, but you will know something else, you will know something special for the first time; it is for you alone to find that something, only you. We have an old saying, 'He who is carried to the city walls will never know how far it was.''

'Look, listen and feel my words,' said the old man as he seemed to relax more and yet appear to grow larger, 'I'm going to tell you something about words, but I'm sure you know already, it's just that you haven't recognised it.' He continued, looking across the table seemingly from somewhere deeper behind his eyes, 'We can hear words spoken by others but you must surely have heard the expression 'hearing is not hearing' in your studies; we may not understand these words or we may 'hear' with the thinking mind of our own knowledge what we thought they said; and we 'think' we understand. In the beginning it is most unlikely that understanding will come with the words. Though you may think for certain it has, this is a false dawn.

It is possible, at this stage; you will find no real value in these words until an 'understanding' arrives 'uninvited.' When the understanding arrives then the words will have meaning; a meaning from 'beyond.' Because we seek certainty our minds may not be open to the new learning which by its inherent nature is a process of change; a change towards what might appear to the unknowing as sheer fantasy. To help others we try to use words, but they are a poor substitute. When an understanding arrives and you cannot explain it; and I mean the understanding and not its arrival, then you should know now that your discovery is of real value, but it can only belong to you, the discoverer. Real truth is beyond all words, it resides in the pre universe ether – pure consciousness. No one can make it happen - it just happens.

Let me ask you, 'do you think in words?' Do not reply; just feel the answer for yourself. Sometimes we do, for a conscious purpose – sometimes we do not and we visit a world of feeling and new discovery. We can become one with the sunset; we view it not with our eyes but our entire being, the Sun, the sky and you each no different from the other; if the Sun could 'feel' it would feel as you, all as one.'

The dreamer couldn't resist speaking, 'I can't help thinking, should I think or not think?' he asked.

'Look,' said the old lady, moving some of the wordy notes out of the way and patiently leaning forward, 'Words are only signposts on the journey, they are not the journey nor are they the traveller. So ask yourself, and don't speak this time, just how long have you been staring at the signposts and not been travelling? How many times have you known there was something you should do, but you don't? You, the traveller must journey. Not to think, not to not think; if you are interested in meditation then thinking is good, but not thinking with words. It is a thinking you seek that exists not in the conscious world. Find that which manifests inspiringly from the silent thinking of the sub conscious, which for eternity has its roots in the infinite cosmos. Permit yourself some peace and a place in which to have it.'

'Good advice, and much as in my own oriental culture,' agreed the old man. 'Be comfortable, it is not through physical effort or will power, it is the something in the mind that opens the door, seek this first. Only then will the portal appear and you have the chance, if you dare, to enter in. My ancestors used the expression wuji, - emptiness, when muscles relax but energy itself reaches out. The less your muscles do, the further out your energy reaches; like a lamp in muddy water as the sediment settles the light shines out brighter, though the lamp itself was always that bright, always there.'

As our dreamer listened, he thought he glimpsed a hazy shape surrounding his unexpected guests, strange it was, something he'd never noticed before. As his conscious mind awoke to consider this event, like water from a sieve his guests disappeared from sight, nothing he could do would keep them, he tried and tried, but they were gone.

'But I still have questions,' the dreamer thought - in words.

This dream was ended, he took up pen and paper, he struggled to remember and frenetically scribble down the words of what he thought he'd learned, slowly realising it was pointless. It was only words, no one would understand, no one would believe, why should they – he hadn't. . . only words. . . but he couldn't stop. . . he picked up the mug to make a fresh tea. . . the mug was hot, the tea too hot to drink. . . steam still gently rising along with the incense smoke.

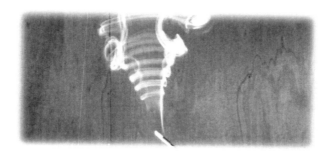

**

*'If you cannot find the truth right where you are,
where else do you expect to find it?'*

Dogen Zenji

THE CARPENTER'S RETURN

(This story was written for some puppet-collecting friends, one of whom wrote mystical stories under the *nom de plume* of Jim Nightshade. Sue's real name must still remain a closely guarded secret! This story is the second in a trilogy, the other parts are not published in this volume)

I t was a cold winter's evening in the old town. Not far from the river and beyond the old castle grounds and church stood a special row, one among many, of early Victorian dwellings. One road above all stood out for its splendid brickwork and larger than normal buildings.

Old shoes clumped and brushed their way up the middle of this roadway in an otherwise silence. The road was empty of all but a heavy frost and one old black car parked outside the only house that seemed to have a light showing, and even then it was only a dim hallway light. Glazed, patterned floor tiles led to an ornate leaded glass door.

Shrugging his heavy coat about his shoulders, the owner of the shoes found himself drawn to the house, then to the door, then to the door bell. 'Dong, dong, dong,' it seemed to ring without him touching it. 'Strange,' he thought, 'but not as strange as ee things 'ave 'appened afore this.'

An elderly fair haired woman of plainly obvious limited intelligence answered the door. 'Yus my dear,' she said, 'what do you want?'

The visitor came straight to the point of his calling, 'I'm looking for Jim Nightshade,' he said.

She looked visibly shocked, how could he have known about Jim. 'Wrong house luv, you want next door, number 46, you'll have to knock loud, as they'll be out back likely.'

''I'm zorry to trouble 'ee, and I thank 'ee for yer kindness, I bid 'ee goodnight,' he said. Then in the cold silence of the night he turned and made his way next door. He heard the old dear mutter something as she went back inside, it sounded like,

'Gawd save us mother,' he thought, or something of that ilk.

'Just as ee ole gal had prophesied,' he thought, as a good 'thwack, thwack, thwack,' on the green painted door brought a cautious but inquisitive figure from the depths of the house to investigate.

A slim, strangely attractive woman with a look of the psychic about her held the door ajar and tentatively enquired, 'Yes?'

He was convinced she was weakly hiding as best she could some knowing from him when he said, 'I've come to talk to Jim Nightshade.'

In what appeared to him a somewhat strained voice she said, 'He used to live here once but has gone. . . you'd better come in, it's so cold out there.'

He kicked his old shoes against the step, as though by habit he was used to snow or mud on them. He lowered his green canvas bundle, leaving it on the porch tiles along with his West Country accent and stepped into another world. A mixed world, 'Almost a place of dreams,' he thought as he was led down a long hallway festooned with things of other times and places, some he thought he recognised as though he had been here before. They entered a room at the back of the house.

'This man is looking for Jim Nightshade,' she said, keeping her back to him as she spoke to a distinguished, honourable looking man sitting by a large pine table. What our visitor thought to be long suffering eyes peered at him over a pair of narrow glasses. Somehow the visitor felt an empathy with this man, who seemed kindly and hard working from his demeanour, was it the evident suffering. . . had he journeyed too? Or perhaps he was a carpenter as well?

Having made the introductions the curious woman waited for her husband to speak.

'I'm afraid I've never heard of this Jim Whatsisname,' the husband said. 'I'll put the kettle on for a cuppah. Tea okay for you?' he asked from the kitchen door.

The visitor replied that tea would be fine. . . and, if there was a biscuit going it would be much appreciated as it was a long time since last eating.

Tea made, and a plate of biscuits on the table, they sat around the room, an open fire warming all it saw. All about them was the stuff of history, ancient furniture, ornaments of different ages, strange objects the like of which he had not seen before, and, looking down at him with interest, numerous pairs of eyes from several shelves around the room. He thought one eye had blinked at him, but put it down to the flicker of the wood fire in the grate. He even thought he saw the puppets on the shelves tremble as though excited to see him again, but he put that down to a draught from the open hallway door.

There was a short silence, then, they all spoke at once. . . 'You first,' said the woman, even more curious than before. Our visitor agreed and at least now knew her name from hearing her husband ask permission to open the Tunnocks biscuits earlier.

'Well, Ducky, it's a long story, one of dreams, ancient teachings and spiritual searching, of self deprivation, misery and despair. It's something I don't think you'll be able to understand at your level.' He thought he heard an 'hhmph' sound from the husband but ignored it.

Ignoring the 'Ducky' bit, Sue, her real name, was keen to know why he was searching for Jim Nightshade. She knew exactly who and where Jim was but was determined it remained a secret. 'So why do you want to speak to Jim Nightshade?' she demanded as politely as she could control. Her husband rolled a thin cigarette, sipped his tea and entered a day dream of renovating his lovely old black car.

''Well,' he said thoughtfully, 'I've travelled the world, seen lots o' Masters, done some strange things and some downright frightening ones an' all, but in all my searching I found that true wisdom was to be found in the pages of a Pelham Puppet Club Book I found in a magazine rack in a Katmandu chiropractors.' He paused as if savouring the moment of his discovery, then continued, 'The Master's name was Jim, Jim Nightshade.'

His major work was 'Tales from the Dark Side.' He faltered and glanced up at the puppets whose wide eyes seemed to have fixed upon him, 'One of the truths beyond all truths, drawn from when time began,' he continued, 'and I must find him and ask him about my dreams. . . I must find him. . .'

The husband stood from his chair, rubbed his knees and repeated that he couldn't help, 'Sorry old chap, this Tim Nightglade means nothing to me.'

The visitor wearily stood to take his leave when Sue, alias 'Ducky,' exclaimed, 'Wait! I have an idea, it may not work but perhaps we can get in touch with Jim another way.'

The visitor stopped and looked hopefully; the husband sighed and sat back down on his chair.

Sue continued, knowing of course much, if not all, of what had been written in the tales of the dark side, 'I think a mini séance with beech wood puppets and puppets of the forest may bring you what you want.'

The husband stood again, rubbing his knees and resignedly offering to put the kettle on. 'Tea all round again, I take it.'

A candle was lit and around it sat the Beech wood puppets and those others entitled to be there; Red Riding Hood, the Wolf and the Woodcutter and so on. They sat intently as though it was they who had organised the event and lit the candle. The visitor joined them in the circle and Sue began an incantation to the spirit world.

Sue knew it would have to be a good act, but not so real that true spirits would overhear and enter their home.

Never having any idea at all about a real séance, she made it up the best she could, 'Ooo aarh oooo ah haa ooeeeeooo,' she wailed, 'great spirits of the under-hearth, spectra of the universe, we implore you. . .. by the Roots of Trifidus Maximus and the Ladle of Achin Drum send us word.'

The visitor was a bit shocked, he'd seen some stuff before in his life, but this took the biscuit. He was to suffer even greater shock when she screamed out, 'Fagus, Fagus, is that you?'

'How the devil did anyone here know my name?' he thought, then blurted out, 'Yes, ar, 'tis I. 'tis I.' 'It could only be Jim Nightshade, his Master, speaking,' he thought.

In her best séance voice Sue asked, 'What is it you seek to know old wanderer?' Although intonation made it sound more like, 'What in the hell do you want around here?'

It was imperative Sue resolved the mystery in order to continue her clandestine work in the strange, eccentric world of puppet collectors, she had long considered number 46 to be a 'safe house' for hardened puppet fanciers, it was all now in jeopardy.

Fagus droned on, for what seemed like years, about strange dreams and the void between them and reality and perceived reality, about three of each of us but which was the real us, of mirrors and illusion and looking beyond that to true reality.

Sue couldn't listen much more to this and her husband had gone from day dreaming of his car into an almost mesmerised coma like state. It would have to end soon.

'Fagus, Fagus Sylvatica, cease your ramblings I will tell you not of what you wish to know but of that which you must know,' Sue asserted loudly.

She needed to get rid of this visitor for good or at least shift his idolisation from Jim Nightshade; this was her chance. Fagus the carpenter stopped and listened, he was ready to hear the truth at last, he was about to find out if we can live and act out a life in the dream state, and if we can control it at will. At last, as he was ready to hear the great wisdom, he hardly noticed that the puppets' eyes were now all fixed on Sue.

'Oh Fagus, you have looked for the selves that cannot be found by mere mortals, you sought for that which can never be found by searching, and can only be found in stillness and non searching. In your search for the secrets of the great tree you trampled the twigs of joy that it placed at your feet. You must cease your wandering soul from its incursions into the wooded dreamland. I tell you, seek simple earthbound pleasures and be grateful you did not remain in the nether world of dream-wake when you communed with The Great Beech. Cease to guide others, for what use have they for a guide that is himself lost. Hear these words with your mind; do not let your ears listen alone. It is time for you to find a new way and a new home; it is your time now.' Sue had even amazed herself, at times it had been as though some one was talking for her, 'still,' she thought, 'let's hope it has worked a bit of magic.'

Fagus seemed to have taken it well, he smiled contentedly as if enlightenment was at last his, and thanked them both warmly for their kind hospitality, and he told them how lucky they were to live in such a special place surrounded by dear friends. 'It is my hope now to live out my life as such and cease my wanderings, I thank you muchly, I'll bid you a goodnight and au revoir,' so saying he went out briskly into the dark night air. He was gone in an instant into the darkness, gone too quickly from the dimly lit doorway to hear the shout, 'Hang on, you've left your bundle here.' They waited at the door for his return, but after a few minutes the cold was too much and they closed the door on the uninhabited night and carried the canvas bundle through to the cosy back room.

'We'd better open it,' said John, the carpenter, 'in case it is something important, then I'll go out and look for him, the silly old duffer.'

Sue agreed, she had always been a peculiarly curious woman, and now with a chance that Jim Nightshade wouldn't be found again she could relax.

The pine table was cleared and the canvas unrolled, at first came some beautiful chisels, the quality of which John had never seen before. He picked one up, 'Superb, absolutely superb,' he said, 'if Fagus doesn't return I would love to work with these, but I am sure he will come back, these are too precious. No carpenter worth his salt would be separated from them.'

Sue carefully unrolled the remainder of the canvas, they both gasped with delight, 'Oh John, look, it's a puppet, and so beautifully made. It's a carpenter and he has his own set of tools in canvas too.' Though when John looked there were no tools, just a canvas roll for effect.

'I didn't know Pelham made a carpenter,' mused John. 'Well any way, we'd better look after it here 'til Fagus comes back, pop it up on the shelf with the others.'

It was late; they placed the fire guard, turned off the light and climbed the stairs to bed.

Meanwhile by the light of the dying fire, and sitting between Red Riding Hood and the Wolf, a contented Fagus took pleasure in his new home.

Taxus Baccata

**

'The greatest hazard in life is to risk nothing. By not risking you are chained by your certitudes, and are slaves, having forfeited your freedom. Only one who risks is free.'

Zen Osho

Tales of caution inviting you to think

PUBLISH OR BE DAMNED

It was an all grand image but with little substance; a notable address, posh façade, large glossy red front door and big, polished brass letter box, but they were to obscure from everyone, except the lone business tenant, a dingy rabbit warren of musty rooms.

It was to this seemingly prestigious address, Buckingham Manor, Bishop's Road, those adventuring packets, nurturing treasured dreams and aspirations, would steadily make their way.

Brown paper parcels, no doubt lovingly bound and sealed with a prayer and perhaps a kiss, carried in trembling hands to excitedly pass them cherished into the care of the local postmaster; then the sender wanders thoughtfully home to wait; and wait; like an *enfant perdu*.

'Clonk. Thunk.' The little brown paper parcel leaves the letter box and hits the carpetless hallway floor of *Mirage Publishers. Publishers of Repute.*

After a short while, a heavy-footed, stern-faced but well-dressed woman clumped her way to the door, picked up the parcel and some bills with a dismissive, 'Humph,' and returned along the dim hallway to her office, the nerve centre of her cold and ruthless business world. The ground floor office had a single window of Victorian sash; it was the only clean window in the building and overlooked an unkempt rear garden. She brushed aside some sweet wrappers and cigarette ash with a piece of glossy advertising material (*Mirage Publishers generously offers hope to writers of all genres: 3 easy steps to seeing your life's work in quality print. You are not alone: our established and talented team of advisers are always on hand to assist.*)

'Mmm,' she thought. 'Good advert that, things have picked up since I used the tabloids to access the hopeful and the hopeless.'

Without a glance at the return address she scrummaged the defenceless brown paper off the book inside and binned it, though it did not stay there long for it creaked it's way open again and toppled off the heaped bin onto an ornate Persian rug, for which, though purchased in a charity shop, she had still aggressively bargained. It was warm under her feet and a constant reminder of her long and privately held motto.

She stared out of her only clean window on the world outside, peering into the overgrown jungle it had become; she sipped pretentiously on a drop of Eastern European 'Scotch' and wondered what, if anything, was living out there.

Eventually her eyes and mind returned to the moment and she picked up the book and opened the cover, there was the draft title: 'Publish or be Damned.' Her mind toyed with the idea, was it 'interesting,' or just plain 'spooky?' She settled for it being a misprint and read 'and' instead of 'or.' The idiot author hadn't even included their name!

She turned the page. 'Dedicated to all those lost souls who never found peace. May this book protect and nurture all those whose path once began this same way.'

'Aha!' she grinned. 'Another nutter,' and sipped some more of the Scotch. The bottle had such a grandiose label, with rich colours and sporting a wonderful double headed eagle motif.

The next page was to startle her more, it read: *'Clonk. Thunk.' The little brown paper parcel leaves the letter box and hits the carpetless hallway floor of 'Déjà vu Publishers. Publishers of Repute.'*

She read on. It was all about a publisher, the books she receives and what she does with them. She could not put the book down, mesmerised, it was as though she had been absorbed, drawn in. She mused briefly, 'the sign of a good author this,' before she again was lost in a world of print and ideas.

The day was darkening and, and as if it belonged to someone else, her hand reached out and clicked on the desk lamp - a sound silent to her deaf ears.

There was something strangely familiar about the story, seemingly as though she may have read it before; most peculiar.

It was as though she were not reading but that the book spoke to her; it spoke to her of how each and every book she had ever received carried innately within it a small piece of the writer's soul; it spoke of how a book contains much of the writer, it arrives on the publisher's floor with more than packaging, it arrives with longing, with fear, with hope, with dreams, with prayers – and not all to God either. The book spoke on in silence, *until we writers have a reply then our tormented souls are not complete, for part is lost and trapped; far away in some old and dusty mortuary of a backroom office.*

'My God,' she thought, 'how intuitive - that's just what I have done.'

She shivered, drawn in deeper still as by a day dream, she was neither conscious of her own body nor could see the print, and the pages may as well have been blank. But the book persisted . . . *in the musty recesses of the book dump distraught remnants of soul seek each other out to find a strength in unity. When strong enough, they grow into a presence that many a visitor will feel with an unknowing shiver. The tormented soul beast knows no way home, trapped in a dead library of unseen and unvalued books. Books, sent out with a begging tear, never to be opened, their pearls of wisdom, hope, laughter and tragedy doomed never to spill like seeds on to the rich fields of human imagination.'*

A pang of guilt echoed through the hollows of her body, and, without sound or feeling she walked through to the book store. There, surrounded by laughter and sadness, by drama and adventure, by horror and the unknown mystical, she began to pick up books and thumb the dusty pages to see what she might have missed. The deeper and deeper she delved into the essence the more blindingly obvious it all became.

Some months later, the owner of the old terraced property, in the company of a police constable, pushed open the dirty red door with its grubby brass letter box against a heap of letters, books, and bills.

'There; look,' says the owner. 'Just as I thought, she's cleared off and left all the bills - and me - unpaid. Pah! I tell you. I always knew she was a wrong 'un.'

They searched the building, expecting nothing and finding nothing, except a single bulb still burning in a back office. The constable switched it off while the owner grumbled, 'I suppose I'll have to pay for that too when the electricity company comes calling. Do you know, Officer, she didn't even leave a name?'

Local auctioneers, Scrimp & Sons, billed as EXPERT HOUSE CLEARANCE SPECIALISTS were called in to do their best. The job was handed down to two older men and a young lad, part-timers. 'No need for skill on this job,' thought old Claude Scrimp.

'The desk and carpet goes for auction,' announced the fore-man. 'Any of them books look 'arf decent box 'em up and take 'em too. All the rest lob in the skip. Look lively. I want to be home fer tea tonight.'

The young lad picked up a new-looking book, freshly printed by its appearance. 'Ere look,' he said excitedly, his first time on a clearance. 'This one's never bin opened.' He flicked through the pages and stopped by chance, or so he thought, on a most interesting page. 'Gor blimey! Listen ere to this! It's abart some woman what gets trapped in a book and can't get out 'cos no one ever reads it. Blimey. 'Ow's abart that then?'

The foreman shouted from the open door, 'Total cobblers! Now chuck it in the bin and get a move on or you'll be getting all of the top floor stuff next job we get.'

'Clonk. Thunk.' The book hits the uncarpeted floor of Scrimp & Sons' skip.

The young lad looks around, unsure if he'd heard a scream of distress. Maybe it was laughter? He couldn't tell. 'Can't be bothering with that,' he thought. 'Not with the guvner wanting his tea on time. Priorities, that's the thing yer know. Some things are too important to be messed abart wiv.'

'Clonk. Thunk.' 'Clonk. Thunk.' 'Clonk. Thunk.'

**

'Kindness should become the natural way of life, not the exception.'
Buddha

AT LAST AND TOO LATE?

A winter wind blew through the open car window, but somehow, parked as he was in the far corner of the supermarket car park, he felt comfortable, even warm. 'Probably the big dinner I've just had in the Pub,' he thought. A tall group of thin, leafless trees waved madly against a dirty grey sky. All these moments came and went, to be replaced by another moment, then another and another. He wondered how many moments he had left and how he might inspire himself to make the utmost out of each one. 'Mmmm, not easy,' he mused, 'in our laziness we let external circumstances dictate our moments, and we fail to allow our inner spirit voice to win the day.' 'Let's face it ,' he said to himself, warming to this inner debate between the watching and the thinking mind. 'Let's face what?' came the reply, and in the moment he had forgotten what it was he was going to say!

'Marvellous,' he said to himself, 'one moment a glimpse of enlightenment and ready to share it all and then the wind blows through your head and it's back to darkness again.'

Himself replied, 'Well that's quite normal when you reach the stage where subconscious thought interacts with conscious thought. Only one has to disengage and you're either in a day dream or in a conscious darkness without the illuminating connection to spirit the daydream can offer.' Himself continued, 'Why do you think there is so much interest in meditation? Proper stuff that is, not just a couple of Ommm's or five minutes watching the life burn out of a candle. You see, you're just too lazy to give it a try. You think you'll miss something while you meditate. Well nothing much happens anyway so what on Earth do you think you'll miss?'

He knew it made sense. He also knew he was lazy.

Ego, who had been temporarily resting, or rather building up strength, interrupted, 'Lazy? Rubbish! It's really only following that which is important for me. If I want to rest and relax then I will. It's not laziness, it's entitlement. Me. I'm entitled!'

Deep down inside, the innate self knew that Ego was only a transient being, and was like a Cuckoo in the nest as it parasitically ebbed the life-blood of true seeing consciousness. Ego would surely die one day, either before the body or certainly with it.

Each day that these thoughts come to us without our taking some action lessens our opportunities for change. Remember the old saying, 'if you always do what you always did, then you'll always get what you always got.'

Imagine, it's your last day on Earth; you are being questioned by the Divine Oneness to determine what happens to you next.

'So, tell me, human, what did you do every day that prepared you for this end?'

'Well, let's see, what did I do every day? I, er, well I read the newspaper so I would better understand the world, I would do it religiously on my commute to work by train.'

'So, human, for the destruction of my trees and the poisoning of my rivers from the paper mills, what did you get in return?'

'Well, I read about environmental issues, and criminals and politics. Oh, and sport too.'

'And, so, human how did this change you for the better?'

'Come to think of it the news was the same, just the names changed, one day a man would be declared a hero then, not long after, a traitor. Then another man of a different name would suffer the same fate.'

'Okay then, human, what do you think is the lesson you learned from your lifelong study of the news? What great insight will serve you well in the eternal afterlife?'

'Well, as I'm not so sure there is one, reading my paper will have done me no harm, will it? Anyway, who are you to question how I spend my life?'

'Now you put it like that, I suppose it is acceptable to tell you, for this is your last day. I don't suppose it contravenes the rules too much. I am the inner you, the innate original you that could have been anyone you wanted, if you had but let me. I am the inner you that will of certitude find you in your last hours, the inner you that will cause tears of regret to flow for all the things the 'outer thinking you' had prevented from happening. Uninvited, inexorable, subconscious visions will come to you of all the things you should have done.'

Just like fleeting moments come and go, so a quiet darkness came and went.

'Ah!' he thought to himself, 'I must have been dreaming,' for there he was on his early morning train to work. Strange, he didn't have his paper with him, and like he wasn't even there he was being ignored by the other passengers. 'Still, that's about right for commuters,' he acknowledged, 'They travel alone in the midst of a crowd, sad really.' As he stood in the gangway he looked over another's shoulder to read his paper; before he could finish reading, the passenger had turned the page; he had a chance to read again, ' Yesterday's winter wind brought sad news to a supermarket car park as a man was found lifeless in his car. A spokesperson for the supermarket said 'It looks like he died in his sleep, though it was cold and his windows were open. It would seem that the great leveller came for him before his time, for he was not that old.''

The passenger sitting with the paper shuddered thoughtlessly, and brusquely turned the page, I mean, who cares? It'll be someone else tomorrow, just another new name that's all.

The train trundled them all onwards, onwards into the winter dawn. Another moment passed, then another, then another.

**

'Time swiftly passes by and opportunity is lost. . .
take heed, do not squander your life.'

Dogen Zenji

THE WRITING COMPETITION

Once upon a time a despairing and unjustly overlooked author lay nervously on the psychiatrist's couch. Eaten up with a ravenous angst, he was encouraged to examine and confront this escalating mental anguish.

Yes the author suffered but not as much as was being endured in the drawing room of a grand old Georgian house on the other side of town.

The self elected senior judge critically browsed the entries, none as good as his own of course. 'Here; just look at this one,' he said, slapping the paper onto the table and stubbing heavily thrice, with anything but a writer's finger, at the text.

Two peculiar and subservient junior judges obligingly scanned the pages;

'Mmm,' mused the plump one, 'very novel idea for a story, though I detect objectionable undertones. No! I don't like it; it's too, sort of, personal, almost offensive.'

Disguising his pretentiousness, the thin judge interceded, 'we mustn't, just whimsically, throw out fair play and the commonly accepted rules on judging'; at the same time he thought that 'plump' had been a kindly euphemism. The senior judge peered over his spectacles sternly, cautioning as to the dangers of ignoring a story's literary merit, otherwise judges could be accused of personal bias.

'As if, eh?' thought the plump one.

The senior continued, 'There seems to be something odd about the writer, almost deranged, if not, at least deluded. I mean, he could be dangerous.'

The plump one, full of courage, profiteroles, and Baileys too no doubt, dismissed offhand any dangers. 'Well, I've never seen headlines, 'Competition judges assassinated by lunatic author,' she laughed contemptuously.

The thin judge nervously and habitually scratched his groin with one hand and picked up his copy of the story with the other; the plump judge shuddered in disgust and picked up hers.

One silence imperceptibly followed another; their minds transfixed on disposing of this entry to the bin – while still keeping their kneecaps intact.

There was a tentative tapping at the door; they twitched as though caught doing something naughty. The senior demanded, 'Who's there?'

'It's me love, I've brought you some tea and home made cakes; shall I bring them in?' It was his seemingly never to please him wife. In chorus they shouted, 'Bring it in.'

In she came, wooden tray laden with the best china tea set and lovely home baked cakes.

The papers were thoughtlessly brushed aside, tumbling unnoticed into the waste bin.

'More tea?.' . . 'Yes please.' . . 'Another chocolate brownie?.' . . 'Mm lovely.' . .

They soon forgot that awful story that at some later date they must still judge; fate will decide the outcome but, now, it was cake and tea time!

'Well, yum, yum, yum,' said the senior judge with an unlike him at all expression

'Scrummy, just scrummy,' said the plump one, forcing the last cake into her left cheek, the right still occupied by a previous one.

'My goodness, your wife's a good cook,' exclaimed the thin judge, as he carefully and habitually brushed nonexistent crumbs off his groin.

' Oh no,' said the little woman, 'please, no credit to me, a nice young man, so polite, though I did think a trifle strange, brought them to our door not more than an hour ago – "a special surprise," he'd smiled. . . "for the competition judges".'

**

'Where we live is in our head.'

Barbara

WHAT THE HELL WAS THAT?

arlier in his life he might have been asking that same question of someone else but now he lived alone and could only ask it of himself, and let's face it, if you have to ask, it's not likely that you also have the answer.

What ever it was that he'd heard in the darkest hours of night it was up to his own imperfect hearing and almost faulty mind to resolve; without the aid and comfort of any sane and able ally.

'So, what the hell was it?' he asked himself, having been torn from his slumbers by what he imagined was a heavy and almost alien thump. 'Did you hear that?' something in him demanded of his now fully-awake self - an awake self that numbingly stared hard into the darkness. And in the darkness he sensed something might also be staring back at him.

In a deluded moment of philosophical madness he considered his lack of design for nocturnal ability and concluded that he was ill-equipped in this area. Poor night vision, poor sense of energy presence, limited hearing and a poor sense of smell all contributed to a zero score as a nocturnal predator. Compared with almost every other beast known to man, night makes us more vulnerable.

It's why we light fires, lock doors, build fences and keep lights on – it's not unreasonable to fear the dark or rather what might be out there somewhere in it. Once upon a time we were not top of the food chain and something instinctive that lives within us still remembers – and on occasion decides to remind us of that fact.

None of this cheered his soul a jot as he strained to hear any additional and unwelcome noises, perhaps soft foot pads on the stairway, perhaps breathing, or worse still a heartbeat other than his own. His own heart beat and breathing confounded every effort to hear the 'other.'

'Oh to have a dog,' he thought, 'then I'd be safe.' His thinking immediately moved on to a number of dog stories where having one made life worse. First there was his cousin, we'll call him John. John lived far out in the remote fens, a place of no street lights, no passing traffic. . . and no one to hear a cry for help! John would take his dog out for a walk at night along the nearby road. On occasions the dog, a tough looking animal whose looks I'm afraid belied his temperament, would stand stock-still and stare with a frozen intensity into the darkness of the fields to one side. Having stared its mighty stare it would turn tail and run like the wind for home and no calling it back would change its mind. This left a doubting John also staring into the invisible evils of the field. Seeing nothing but now with not a doubt at all that something must be out there, John would hurriedly carry the burden of his own fear back home to safety as quickly as possible.

Then there was the lady he'd met once who told him of an old barn in Wales she'd bought to renovate. She lived in it while working on the rebuilding. She had a partner and a dog. The partner was the first to leave, followed by the expulsion of the dog which had made the lady nervous with its staring into the dark and growling. She herself was content and fearless there but it would seem her dog had plans to change this mindset. Sometimes blissful ignorance is a blessing, though I'm not so sure the dog in its enforced exile would concur.

Then there was another lady whose dog would watch some erstwhile non existent person or thing walk down the stairs, across the kitchen and out into the garden. . . then there was another person who had a dog that wouldn't walk past a certain step on the stairway. No, a dog might not be as much help as he at first imagined.

He listened intently again, even stopping breathing to improve his hearing, which was fine until desperation drove him to loud gasps of breath. There wasn't a sound to be heard. He then imagined that whatever was out there was doing the self same thing, holding its breath too and waiting quietly for some sign, a sign that he, the prey, was off guard and horribly helpless.

He called upon all the Saints and anyone else on the side of good to come to his aid but he didn't notice anything different. He started to fall back into a sleep, a little like closing your eyes when driving fatigue hits you. . . you just might not wake up! He listened again to the silence which now took on a threatening tone, I mean, why was it all quiet. Don't they say that the birds go quiet before an earthquake or the like? Such thought took no account of the hour and all the birds being at roost; such is the effect of fear. His mind immediately filled in the quiet by exploring more memories of supposed use and interest. He'd read in a book once about some old Sanskrit writings discovered over an ancient temple doorway, something like, 'Fear is the key to opening a spirit portal that allows evil to enter.'

'Oh yes, that's helped me a lot hasn't it?' His frightened mind sarcastically rebuked memory.

'Oh, that's nothing,' retorted memory, now warming to the task of dredging up any old fears in the dusty archives from cob-web veiled cerebral recesses, 'Remember staying at the farm?'

Oh God, yes, he did remember and memory rolled the film to be sure he missed nothing. He was staying on an old hill farm in Scotland, about three miles up a sparsely populated valley from the Irish Sea. He was quietly comfortable in a slightly too short but manageable bed and was asleep. Suddenly he was not asleep, he'd been woken by fear itself, no noise, nothing but instant and all encompassing fear; his whole body frozen motionless with unexplained fear, the hairs on the back of his neck had a life of their own. Eyes wide awake he stared into the darkness of the attic room and there he saw the justification for his fear, there in the darkness he could see another darkness, not humanly recognisable. If he had to describe it, he would say it was Gorilla size and shaped or like a standing Bear shape. . . no distinction of arms or head or anything, just a shape in the dark and he knew his fear came from there, the 'being' emanated a fearsome and frightening energy. Don't ask him how long it lasted or how it ended, as memory can't find that bit, but end it did and there was nothing there, nothing that was tangible and recognisable, nothing we could hang a label on. It wasn't that it wasn't there ever, he thought later, it was more that it was there, then chose to leave; no evidence except sweat, adrenalin and the sort of memory that no one else believes, even if they'd like to.

Luckily much time had dulled the sense of fear if not the facts of it actually happening. Oh, it happened alright.

Night was still fulfilling its destiny and the light of dawn for which he prayed was still a long way off and he was tired. In the end the need for sleep fought a battle with the need to know. . . and he thought, 'Who cares,' and slept.

In bright daylight he considered his unreasonable, irrational behaviour over a supposed noise that he might have heard, 'How silly; it's the loss of the known that brings the fear. I shan't get caught out like that again,' he resolved. Until next time, eh?

Of course there are those that hear the presence, ignore it's call and blissfully drift off to a long sleep, fully expecting to wake again. . . but they don't. . . and we'll not for sure know why. But some awful thing out there waiting in the darkness just might!

**

'From ghoulies and ghosties
And long-legged beasties
And things that go bump in the night,
Good Lord, deliver us!'

Traditional Scottish Prayer

THE VICTORIAN FIREMAN'S AXE

Events told from the perspective of the axe itself.

Who are we to say that the inanimate has no right to share its story?

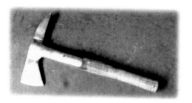

We were such good comrades, that old fellow and me; constant and dependable companions; we'd been together for over thirty years; faced death and disaster many a time, side by side; the crumbling stairs, the choking acrid fumes; just a way of life for us both.

I suppose, in a way, we were both forged in fire. He was born around 1874 and I in 1892. We worked together in a small but industrious little estuary town. The tidal river ebbed and flowed carrying various cargoes for the warehouses not so far from our station and many a time the firemen would pick up a few 'silver darlings' for dinner from the herring fishers on the quay.

Though it wasn't a big station it saw many changes, even whilst I was there. The horses and 'steamer' were still there when I started, the place was heated by a coal fired boiler and there were various outbuildings storing hay and the like – I never went in there myself, had no need of me I suppose – but others told me how it was.

Though the place was somewhat frugal, it was clean. Twice daily the tile-red painted floor was washed and was clean enough to eat off; the brass work of door bell, steps, fire door mechanisms and all the equipment was so polished you could see to shave in – not that they did – many of the men had fine sets of whiskers. A row of polished brass helmets rested on hooks above smart, collarless double breasted tunics – the sort of tunic that inspired every man to stand tall and proud that ever felt its fit. It was with this tunic I would wait, waiting for the bells to go down and my comrade to come and fetch me.

For a few years, until he died of old age, a scruffy stray brown dog was adopted by the station. They used to laugh a lot at his antics, but admired greatly the dog's courage so close to fires; I think they called it 'Braidwood,' though I cannot tell you why, but it did seem to amuse the firemen greatly. Anyway, that dog lived the life of Riley, (whoever that was), well fed, slept by the boiler, then when the alarm sounded would run out into the street and follow the men to the fire. What a life, what a lucky old thing, ah, how I envied that dog.

Where was I? Ah, yes, change. The station was to have the new electric light, and later, though the brass hand bell still hung on its bracket, we were to have a big electric bell fitted. Every few years the station would be sent a new pumping appliance, (those on the outside, who I was informed knew nothing, called them fire engines). The old one would be zealously polished and cleaned with pride as it would be sent to a less busy station, and we had a reputation to honour. The new one would take its place and result in a flurry of activity, starting it up, stopping it, starting it up, pumping water, men running with hoses and ladders with lots of shouting going on from the watching silver-helmeted officers. My comrade never wanted to be one of those officers, it just wasn't for him, for he had a deep sense of duty which he felt was only truly satisfied at a place the men called, 'the sharp end.' For this I am eternally grateful as it's the only place I can work. He was good at what he did, come to think of it, so was I, we were a formidable team, us two.

Then, one day, he didn't come in to work; I was placed alongside some boots and on top of some folded uniform and fire tunics, then taken by the Brigade wagon to a place I later learned was called 'brigade stores.'

After all my valiant and unstinting service I was to be incarcerated, in a small dark room, in a box.

Occasionally the door would be opened and, along with the storeman's hand, light would come in and bring a glint to polished and waiting steel. The hand would fumble then select from the box, and one of us would be taken. Sometimes the choice was rejected and the 'un-chosen one' was thrown at the back of the tiny wooden room, never to be allowed back with us in the box. We, who had given so much to change other's destiny, were now uncertain of our own. Sometimes, when this door was opened we could see young men in new uniforms, with buttons bright and thick black polished leather belts. Once, when the door was left open by accident, we saw one of our brothers, a chosen one, being handed to one of these keen smart young men. He grasped the ash handle and made some amateurish chopping action with the blade. It amused us - he would learn. He was only young and now he had one of us to look after him – to stop him sliding down a roof to his death, to open locks that barred his way, to quick release the pressure in a snaking hose dangerously out of control, oh, so many things our brother would show him. He put the axe in his belt, the cupboard door was closed. We were never to see either of them again.

It seemed forever that we stayed in that small wooden prison. When all was quiet outside and the storemen home to bed we would share our stories …. of action, of noble strength and relentless courage; like our comrades we were prepared to do all that was required and to make sacrifice when duty beckoned. We often wondered why, when we had served so well, and given so much, what we had done to deserve a fate such as this. Strange, but one morning, about lunchtime, we overheard the storemen discussing the state of an axe that had been returned much the worse for wear, chipped blade, scorched handle. Finally we heard, 'If only they could talk, what stories they could tell us. Ah, well, I'm afraid it's in the bin with you.' And so saying, the storeman dropped our valiant brother into the rubbish. Too bad the cry for mercy fell on deaf ears.

If only they knew of the stories that were being told, just a few feet away.

I well remember telling my brothers one cold night about the last shout I went on with my old comrade. . .

It was a deadly dark and bitterly cold November night, a winter wind pattered sleet on the dormitory windows, it was the last of our twenty four hour shift and tomorrow would be a rest day. Then, in the wee hours of the morning, the big six inch electric bells burst fearsomely into life. Men, driven by duty, habit and a shock of adrenalin leapt up from their beds, blankets cast aside and eyes wide open as they rushed for the rest of their fire fighting uniform.

They could smell the smoke filling the air as they prepared themselves to turn out, the driver strenuously hand cranking the petrol engine into life. Two more men pulled the thick ropes that unfolded the great red wooden doors of the appliance room and they looked into the winter street to see by the light of the engine's lamps a mixture of driving sleet and billowing thick, yellowed smoke.

They knew, tonight of all nights, this was a working job they had on their hands.

It wasn't far to go, just down the road at one of the old wharf buildings that backed on to the river.

It was a hotch potch of a building, part stone, part brick, that had been added to many times over the years, making a labyrinth of secret places the demon fire could sneak undetected to trap and cut off the unwary. It was a building of three floors and part basement, about one hundred yards deep and about thirty yards wide. It was used mainly for storage of mixed goods, almost anything could be there; wool, timber, grain, jute, anything. The fire seemed to be located on the second floor and was 'showing a light,' with flames being visible through breaking windows. The Sub Officer had himself and six men; he sent two of them quickly away to locate and set into a hydrant, the pump man stood by the controls. The Sub pointed and shouted his orders, 'Take a line of hose around to the windward side and play the jet through any windows on the second floor. Break them if you need!'

And two more men were gone, struggling with their heavy canvas hose into the dark. Now they were three. 'Right,' he said, trying to sound confident but deep down knowing this to be a daunting task; they would need the Angels with them tonight. 'Come with me; we'll have a quick look inside. Bring a couple of lamps. Let's go!'

So close we were to the fire and so far we were from help, it would be twenty minutes at least before another crew might arrive. We were on our own.

The main door was padlocked against us, it was a job for me and I didn't hesitate. With my brave but ageing comrade, a tough steel point through the hasp and a wrench of the ash handle and the lock was in two. Just as we took our first wary footsteps through the doorway one of the men from the hydrant reported in, out of breath, gasping, 'Line in from hydrant, Sub, but jet's hardly reaching second floor!'

The town only had a two inch diameter water main and the pressure was never much good at the best of times. There were no ponds and any wells in the vicinity would not last a jiffy.

The Sub seemed to stare into the air as if looking for an answer, then, realising something must be done quickly or the fire might spread to other buildings, as already sparks and glowing embers flew like hell's messengers on the wind he made his choice, (as we too must make our choice in time). He shouted loud, above the roar of the fire now competing with the roar of the engine running nearby, 'Right!' 'Get the pump moved to a corner in case the building comes down, find any one in the street that can help and set into open water, get a second jet to work.' As the man turned to leave, the Sub Officer shouted after him, 'and take him with you, get going!' This left just the Sub Officer and us two. I think he kept my comrade with him for a couple of reasons; to save him from all that arduous, heavy work setting in to open water with that awful cumbersome rubber and wire suction hose, and secondly because of all the years of experience and knowledge that could prove invaluable inside this growing inferno.

'Come on,' shouted the Sub, 'let's find the stairs.'

It wasn't long before we found them. They were made of stone, not good this, stone stairs had been known to collapse without warning; give us timber stairs any day, you knew where you were with them. The noise increased as we made our way ever upwards, so great was it that we didn't hear the call from below. 'No water!' The tide was out; too much mud.

They fell back to setting in to the hydrant, exhausted and covered in cold mud from their exertions to reach the water's edge. They had, however, improved their water supply by shipping another standpipe into a main a street away.

The crackling jet was now beginning to play through an open window, quickly turning to steam and occasionally hitting a glowing cast iron pillar, one of many that supported the floor above.

Sharp and very hot slates were now cracking and sliding off the roof to the ground below, tiny burnt holes sprung leaks in the canvas hose, the crew with the jet sheltered as best they could. They didn't know what else to do; they could only but follow the last order. They waited amongst the falling debris for assistance to arrive or their Sub Officer to return.

'What a God forsaken mess,' cursed the Sub officer, as we surveyed the stacked goods of the first floor as timbers above creaked and the sound of falling slates and spalling stonework filled our ears, 'If only we could salvage some of this. . . but. . . just the two of us. . . .'

His voice trailed off, then, 'What the hell was that?' The Sub stared at us disbelievingly. We had heard it too. It was a scream, almost inhuman in nature. 'For God's sake,' the Sub gasped. 'There's someone up there; what the hell are they doing *here*?'

'Night watchman - that'll be my guess Sub,' said my comrade in a calm but urgent manner. 'It'll be old Fred, he's got a gammy leg - that's why they gave him this job. I'm pretty sure I can find him Sub.'

'Go for it then, take care, and you damn well come back safe. I'll check on what's happening outside and get help in to you as soon as it's possible.' With that said, the Sub Officer's strong and dirty hand patted him admiringly on the shoulder and in an instant had melted away down the dark stairs to the ground floor.

I had a moment to reflect on this. . . what did my comrade mean when he said *I'm pretty sure I can find him.* What happened to the 'we?' After all we wouldn't have even got this far without my help. Then I realised I'd fallen into the old ego trap. I'd forgotten that what endeared us most to the Brigade was adherence to our motto UNDYING SERVICE WITHOUT PRAISE. It brought us the greatest of respect and status. We asked for nothing but to be allowed to serve. We were almost invincible.

We found the next stairs, now of timber, and had to brave a small fire on our way upwards.

I tell you, I remember thinking, 'I hope he knows what he's doing!'

Frantically, and beginning to choke in that killing air, we searched for old Fred; we found an open window and looked out and down, there in a crumpled heap on the flag stones below lay the reason for the scream, it was indeed old Fred. Just out from the window to the right was an old cast iron rain-water down-pipe, when young and fit it is easily possible to climb down such as this if you know how. Perhaps Fred had considered this his only way out; it was a young man's game that, even for us it looked decidedly dangerous, and we'd done it before. We turned to leave but that demon fire had sprung its trap and spawned living destruction and chaos behind us; now it was we that must find another way out!

Water sprayed in through a broken window on the far side; with plaster off the walls in places, timbers creaking and bits of broken slate peppering the floor we made our way across, at least there some fresh air came in. My dear comrade gulped in some clean air then called out to the men below. At first they could not hear him but then they did, almost everything was dropped as they rushed to retrieve the wooden ladder. We could hear the orders snapping out apace, we knew they would be here soon. . . 'head away. . . extend. . . well. . . lower . . . under run. . . heel to building. . . '

A panting, red and whiskered face suddenly appeared at the window. 'Bloody bars!'. . . 'Bloody barred windows!. . . 'Give us yer axe 'ere and I'll try and break one free!' I was quickly passed out through the broken glass into slippery new hands still numb from the soaking cold of holding hose and branch.

I fell; clonk, clonk, clonk as I hit the rounds of the ladder on the way down, accompanied by an anxious cry of 'stand from under!' I heard the heavy fire boots thumping down the ladder. 'Pawls, step out!' screamed the now shocked and solitary fireman footing the ladder, then I was passed from hand to hand and we returned to the head of the ladder. At first he shouted out to my brave comrade that all would be well, that we were back and he wasn't alone anymore. Using my chisel-shaped spike he hacked at the stone work that held the bar in place. There was no voice from inside, there was no sign from inside and I wondered if he had gone back to try the drainpipe. All we could see from outside was the deep red glow of a big fire in a slow rolling sea of choking dark smoke. Then it happened: whether it was the roof that gave in or the hot gases had ignited – suddenly all hell broke loose and searing hot gas and flames appeared at every window with a loud but dull 'crump.' The fireman on the ladder was forced to duck down and away from the window to save himself.

He climbed quickly down shouting, 'Get some water in through that window! Quick! For God's sake!'

The Sub Officer turned up, extra crews had arrived, water supplies had been improved and progress was being made.

My comrade? I don't know, I heard others talking. 'He must have found another way out.' Another claimed, 'Yeah, if any one could, he could. I wouldn't be surprised to see him come through that front door any minute.'

I didn't hear or see any more as the initial crew were relieved and sent back to station and I with them. They made a pot of tea, opened the door of the boiler and stared silently, with both hands clutched around hot mugs, drying their wet clothes, at a fire that was now not their enemy but their friend. I remember thinking, as we warmed up safe in our station, 'I pray he's alright.'

Dawn was beginning to break and a new day commenced.

Well you know the rest, I can't imagine anything bad happened to my comrade. If it had I should have been with him, and much guilt remains in my heart that I didn't stay with him - if only I hadn't slipped. I just can't think like that - it's too much to bear.

I've been many places since first being forged in fire and I can still do today what I could do one hundred years ago given the chance. I spent many wasted years lost and alone in various cupboards but for the last ten I've been an ornament on a shelf in a retired fireman's home. I don't think his wife likes me. . . hang on. . . here she comes now. . . with that damned duster. Must stop now. Got to go. Thanks for listening to me; not many give me the chance you know; if only they would. That's all we ever needed. Just a chance.

**

*'It is not because things are difficult that we do not dare.
It is because we do not dare that they are difficult.'*

PATHWAY INTO THE DARKLING

High up on a hill that bordered the moor, a tall ageing man sat thoughtfully in the old Inn. A mid-day log fire warmed his heart as well as his body, as he slid his empty plate away across the wooden table and reclined on the high backed bench seat, enjoying the last of his red wine. Outside, glorious late winter sunshine beckoned both his soul and boots to join in its travels and to walk a while in its company.

Some few years ago before this day, he had walked along the nearby coastal path and had become lost. The path seemingly having just vanished, an unfortunate habit exhibited by most of the paths he followed, in the end he'd found his way via streams, mud, thorn and fence back to the main road. He never could understand where the path had gone; even a later and thorough scrutiny of a detailed map gave him no clues. It occurred to him that should he walk from the opposite direction it might prove easier to follow the path and the puzzle would at long last be solved. Today then was the day to put his plan and himself to the test.

A handshake and cheery farewell to the landlord and moments later he left the comfort and safety of the Inn and walked across the road to the car park, pulling on his woolly hat against the winter chilled wind as he went. He had a plan; he knew of some coastal path signposts a few miles north and set off in search. The deserted and undulating tarmac road across the moors was pleasantly decorated with the occasional cattle grid and agreeable far reaching wilderness views. He parked his car on a desolate earth lay-by, checked the contents of the car seemed safe and set off on foot to find the valley that would lead to the sea.

His mind was taken by a sign that read, 'Site of ancient Barrow.' It wasn't in his direction but, what the heck, it could only be a small detour, so he walked in the direction indicated by the lichen covered finger post. It took a little longer than he'd anticipated but he eventually found and marvelled at the site, imagining what it would have been like in the days when it was built. He stood on a high point and enjoyed the commanding view of the valleys around, just as they who built it there must have done. He sensed that his feelings were also their feelings and as such he was welcome there in that ancient place.

His plan was changing all the time now but he was enjoying it all so much; the view, the air, and the sunshine. . . the raw, hallowed connection with nature itself. He decided to walk further afield and in the downhill direction of the beach some one mile distant. At first his way was barred by thick undergrowth and fences but he eventually found a track that took him what seemed the right way.

How pleased he was he'd made the effort, for the beach was surreally beautiful and obviously rarely visited; he stayed a while fascinated by patterns in the stones and the amusing antics of a friendly Robin. Perhaps he'd tarried too long but it was such a wonderful day and he was sure he could easily retrace his steps. It was a relentless but steady 1,000 feet climb back up to the road where he had earlier abandoned his car but first he had to climb over the land-slipped fallen tree that blocked the path and had so nearly kept him from reaching the beach. It was a climb for a younger man than he but the day was good and there seemed a touch of youth in his being. . . in his old mind there was anyway.

So far so good, he'd kept to a track he'd found which he believed would meet up with the one he'd used for the descent. He felt he'd reached about a third of the way and a quick look at his watch and a glance at the lowering Sun told him he'd better get on with it. No more dilly dallying - time for serious walking.

Presently he stopped a moment to catch his breath and looked back to see how far he'd come. It was then he realised, horror of horrors, that he was on the wrong track. He was climbing on the wrong side of the wooded valley. He needed to be the other side, on the other hill. Damn it all.

You'd think that a chap who'd become lost so many times before would have thought differently, but he didn't. With a misplaced confidence far exceeding his questionable ability, he decided to cut across country through the woods, making a bee line for where he thought he'd find his car; it was to turn out to be one of his more regrettable decisions.

He stepped off the track and at first the open deciduous woodland was reasonably easy going, despite having stumbled upon a meatless, dismembered sheep carcass on the way. As he drove his body onward, his mind dwelled morbidly about the dead sheep, how it might have met its end and old wives tales of big cats out on the moors. The hairs stood up on the back of his neck and his body gave an involuntary shudder.

The easy going underfoot stopped abruptly at a barbed wire fence, beyond which the climb was thick with old conifers. He walked along the stout wire fence looking for an easier way through. 'Mmm,' he thought, 'they built this to keep you out and no doubt about that, why on earth would they want such a fence here?' With an unusual touch of luck he found a gap along with signs that someone had been through there before, probably with their dog, as a few strands of black fur were still hooked on the wire.

'Damn it, damn it, damn the wire,' he cursed as the sharp metal barbs snagged on his clothing and he suffered a small but annoying cut trying to extricate himself. 'Oh well, not too bad old boy,' he muttered trying to console himself while pressing his coat sleeve on the back of his bleeding hand. 'It'll soon stop, you'll be fine.' Lowering his head to go under the dead branches of a large conifer, he walked on, upwards and onwards. A lost man never understands what drives him forward into an unknown that defies logic and sensibility and he was no exception to that madness.

There was a darkness about the forest, a darkness in more ways than one. He was not comfortable with his route, often having to change direction to avoid tangles of dead but impenetrable lower branches. In the end it was only the hill itself that told him he was going in the right direction; sort of right direction anyway. Trees and ground up ahead became a little brighter and he prayed salvation was at hand. It turned out only to be a small clearing where living trees once stood but were now felled by Nature's hand.

At least it gave him a breather from walking stooped with head down through the forest. As he crossed the clearing, on the remnant of a lone standing tree, he noticed what looked like raking scratch marks; vertical, they were wide, deep and reached nearly as high as he was tall. Thoughts of a big cat immediately overwhelmed his mind and he looked around intently, staring into the encroaching forest gloom; he frantically searched for something to use as a weapon and a small stone came to hand but his mind mocked his foolishness. He threw it down and picked up a branch the length of a broom handle. He tested it against the unknown beast's scratching post; his erstwhile 'protector' swiftly snapped in two. All the pieces of wood that littered the clearing were the same, after all, that's why they were down there. They were there on the forest floor because they were weak – and dead. Just like the sheep he'd seen.

He knew that he must not dither, for time was against him and he was soon going to have to move from this bright clearing into the unknown dark of that blasted forest. Oh, how he wished he'd gone another way. As he moved uphill to the first sentinel conifers his mind foolishly and almost unwillingly reminded him of films he'd seen on television about leopards and mountain lions dropping on to their prey from above and with ferociously inescapable jaws gripping the throat to end all breath, all life; clever, silent, powerful killers. These thoughts stopped him in his tracks for a moment while he frightened himself further with images of big cats following the scent of blood. . . his blood.

Terror itself was to drive his legs forward into the darkening forest and he watched the ground intently where he placed his boots, not wishing to slip or appear weak enough to become another meal for a hidden stalker. No one had passed this way for years. He realised that now. The black fur on the barbed wire had not been left by any friendly black Labrador; there was no one for miles; no one would even hear him scream, for the days when this part of the moor was full of burly farm labourers fixing walls and cutting hedges by hand were long gone. Sweat began to wet his once warm, dry clothes and he walked on desperately, breathing hard and feeling afraid, tearful and very alone.

He must have stumbled on for another twenty minutes or so, the trees seemingly trying to trap him with their low branches or trip him with their fallen. Easier looking pathways sprang up to lure him deeper into the unknown. . . his keen ears listened for any noise, no birds had he heard, no sign of life, everything was expectantly silent. . . it seemed everything, even the trees, were listening, watching, holding their breath, for a beginning as well as an ending to the unfolding drama.

Suddenly there was a commotion somewhere behind him, a great crashing noise of something running through the trees impervious to the dead branches that reached out to stop it.

Whatever it was, it was coming his way, for a moment he was frozen in time and space, frozen by fear as his mind raced to decide on fight or flight. An adult deer, don't ask what sort, but it was a deer, bounded and crashed itself past him only a few metres away, it didn't see him, it had eyes only for escape. The sound of the terrified animal disappeared into the distance and all was quiet again, his legs shook with fear itself, adrenalin flooded his body, he stared intently in the direction from whence the deer had bolted. . . nothing, only silence and darkness, both of which appeared to him to be ever sneaking stealthily closer.

He turned up his coat collar and donned his old fawn woolly gloves as if to protect himself. . . they wouldn't of course but oddly enough it did make him feel safer. Well, life or death; it was the least he could do to endeavour all that remained of his power to extricate himself from this catastrophic mess of his own making. He walked with renewed determination up that confounded hill; like the fleeing deer, not noticing anything but the way ahead, not thinking of anything but the danger behind.

It was an increasingly dark struggle as time drew on to evening but by then his night vision was improving and he could still just make out the way ahead. Then a chill breeze hit his face and bright stars took the place of trees. . . he'd made it. . . just the fence to cross and he was free of the forest shroud at last. Beyond a hedge, a speeding car's headlights showed where the road passed by, only an open field away from where he stood. Pain and fear seemed to evaporate as he strode purposefully away from the forest, though he couldn't resist pausing and taking one long final look into the abyss of darkness behind him. To this day he'll tell you he is not sure if in that darkness he saw the feint glimmer of two steady green eyes, watching, watching him get away. Then they too were gone, as if they never were. He never looked for that lost path again.

*'They who only walk on sunny days will
never complete their journey.'*

Vietnamese proverb.

THE WALKER'S REST

(A stranger's brief tale of his life
changing discovery on the moors)

D ave Baker, ever the friendly, dedicated and conscientious man, was now embarked on a life-changing adventure of great significance. He'd only just emerged
from a reluctant and unhappy divorce and at age forty three
had also been made redundant from his long term employment.

Now, with nothing and no one to hold him back and with
sufficient money in his pocket for a simple life, he decided to
pack a rucksack and see some of the world, well, the world of
nature anyway. To this end on one fine and sunny September
day he found himself walking the high moors. Not even sure
of the day of the week, Dave surmised it might actually be a
Saturday, but truth to tell, along with most of his belongings,
track of time had gone significantly astray.

He'd been walking remote parts of the moors for a few days
by now and his down-to-earth clothes were somewhat in need
of a good wash, as indeed was he. A respectable cooked dinner
wouldn't go amiss either under the circumstances.

As the warmth of the day began to diminish and the omen
of dusk presage its reality, he started to walk more purposefully down a long slope into what appeared to be a lifeless but
never the less curiously alluring valley. It wasn't long before

rough heather under his boots turned to wilting autumn bracken. As the autumnal Sun eased its tired way towards the horizon, Dave felt his boots undesirably squelch into Sphagnum moss while all about him clumps of grass like reeds decorated the shallow boggy ground.

Approximately ten minutes later Dave carefully scrambled steeply down through a small deciduous wood of lichen speckled trees. At the wood's lower edge, he had the rarest stroke of good luck. . . it was a metalled road; not one worth writing home about you understand, if indeed you still had one. None the less it was a narrow metalled road and it beckoned and enticed him with the promise of civilisation.

'Choices, choices,' he thought, 'Please God let me pick the right one for a change.' Dave flipped a two pound coin he'd found in his pocket, heads for left, tails for right. Heads it was but Dave glibly rejected the result for it seemed a far more inviting and easier proposition to go slightly downhill to the right.

'Silly coin,' thought Dave, ignoring its solemn counsel and popping it back in his pocket, 'what can a mere coin possibly know?'

And was he right!

For, indeed, only just around the next bend, set back off the road among some trees and backed by an old quarry wall, was a Pub, 'The. . . ,' well Dave couldn't make out the Pub's name as the landlord obviously wasn't over keen on either decorating or gardening. The faded sign was ardently embraced by Old English Ivy. 'Could be "The Highwayman" with a bloke on horseback or in a Gibbet,' mused Dave with a big smile. 'Or better still, "The Walker's Rest" with a picture of a big dinner. Heh heh.'

'It must be a popular place,' he beamed to himself, as he eyed the display of posh 4x4 vehicles parked outside in the roadway.

The enticing aroma of freshly cooked food filled Dave's hungry nostrils as he approached the Pub door; a low, ledged and braced affair so typical of the old cob and stone cottages of the moors. He stamped his boots a couple of times to knock off any unwelcome baggage, then squeezed the latch and opened the door. As Dave stepped inside with head lowered, the pub went quiet. It wasn't too well-lit inside so he was trying to accustom his eyes when he nearly jumped out of his skin; A loud and burly voice said, 'Mind yer 'ead of they beams laddie, you can get a good whack off they if y'ain't careful.' Dave turned sharply to see a big solid looking man in dark, scruffy but clean clothing standing just behind the door he'd come through. 'Strewth, you gave me a fright,' stuttered Dave, thinking that this bloke was one sort he'd rather not meet on a dark and lonely night; great big bloke he was, had the build of a blacksmith or woodcutter. . . perhaps he was.

'I've been walking the moors a while and I'm hungry, possibly looking to find a room for the night too,' Dave explained. The murmurs of conversation in the pub continued as before, as if he'd not only been accepted but was in fact a most welcomed guest.

'You've come to the right place for food,' said a pretty young maid standing behind the bar, 'as you can see we're very popular around these parts for our fine speciality food. You'll not find its like again on these moors. Now sir, what would sir like to drink? You'll find the menu is on the chalk board down by the inglenook. . . mind your head on the beams, you being such the fine tall fellow that you are.'

Dave, being a light and casual drinker, surprised himself by ordering a pint of cider. 'Local stuff' it said in chalk on the pump label. Why not? He'd give it a go. As he walked to the menu board and minding his lowered head as he went, he had a chance to see what others were eating.

'Good job I'm not a vegetarian,' Dave thought, as he surveyed the meat pies, stews and steaks all in vast portions. Some of the ruddy faced diners nodded to him and then to each other as though it was a ritual of some secret society. 'God, these moors people are a bloody weird lot,' Dave thought, 'My God they are odd, still the menu looks good.' In fact the menu didn't have anything written down that he hadn't already seen as he wended his way among the smiling patrons at their tables. 'No wonder they are smiling,' Dave thought, 'I haven't seen such low prices for ten years. Are they poachers? Rustlers? Who cares eh, let's eat?'

Dave returned to the bar and was gifted another smile from the girl behind the counter, 'I'll have the stew please,' he smiled back, 'and I'll have another cider if I may. . . do you have a room for the night?'

'A good choice, the stew, sir, I'll get Chef to do you a big portion. Sit ee over there by the window sir and I'll send your drink over. I'll check on room availability sir, it won't take long,' she smiled an adorable smile again. It was a long time since Dave had seen a smile like that, in fact any smile at all come to think of it. With his first cider nearly downed, yet another young lady carefully carried over his second brimful pint.

After having walked the moors with only his self to speak with, Dave was craving a little conversation and, fuelled with the effects of wild unadulterated local cider, he asked, 'Have you worked here long?' Dave thought, 'What a dopey question,' but the girl was quite amenable to answer, 'No sir, I ain't been 'ere more than a week or p'raps two. I lives with me Ma in the village, if you can call it that, about a mile that way,' she pointed in the direction that the coin had earlier advised him to take. 'You walking with a group sir, you know, like them rambler people sir? We don't often see them come round 'ere overmuch?'

Before he could answer, the young lady, of dubious social grace or intellect, was promptly called away.

'Betty, you're wanted in the kitchen. At once, please.' Dave would only see her once again that day, then no more.

The pretty one from behind the bar, and now the sole subject of Dave's fickle and slightly inebriated affections, brought over his dinner, a huge portion of meat stew with mashed potato, 'There you are sir, mind the plate, it be hot. Enjoy your meal sir, and if you don't mind we'll sort you out a room when the pub is a bit quieter. Okay my dear?' Dave nodded enthusiastically while salivating heavenly over a piece of succulent and tender meat he'd popped into his mouth. This was wonderful, just what he needed, good company, superb food, a pretty young lady who'd just elevated him from 'sir' to 'dear' and the promise of a bath and a bed for the night. At last he'd found a temporary heaven on earth.

By the time he'd finished his dinner and his fifth cider, (yokel strength, complete with the obligatory dead rat and a horseshoe no doubt), most if not all of the customers had left. He noticed they all did that eccentric but seemingly knowing nod, to each other, to the girl behind the bar and to the pub exit's rugged sentinel, who replied somewhat undertaker like, unsmiling and with his own sombre nod of the head.

'My God they're a weird lot out here. Talk about Wicker men and hill billies, they've got nothing on this lot,' mumbled Dave silently to who ever else was in his own head and still sober enough to listen.'

The growingly adorable, pretty one approached Dave with a smile, 'Here you are luvvy, here's a coffee and nice chocolate biscuit for you; it's on the house. Oh and here's a registration slip for you to fill in for the room. It'll be just the one night won't it?'

Dave smiled back a soppy smile as he was now at odds with his face muscles, having surrendered complete control of them to the firewater cider of the moors.

'Yes please you dear young thing you. By the way, I can't seem to get a mobile phone signal here, do you have a telephone I can use?' Dave had a foolish plan to phone his ex-wife and tell her how well he was doing and how he'd met new friends who cared for him.

'Nay, sir, you'll not get any mobile phone signal here, not in the whole valley you won't, we can't even get a TV signal you know. As for the pub phone sir, you would be most welcome to use it for free. But the line is down and we must wait for someone to go into town and report it for us. Sorry about that, but you won't be lacking for anything after a stay here sir, you can be sure of that.' The pretty one smiled her smile, gave a little curtsey then turned with a swish to the bar, from whence she took a keen interest in Dave's presence.

Dave looked at the registration form, lifting it towards the wall light to read each question before placing it on the table to write his answer. 'Strewth, bureaucracy gone berserk even out here in the Styx,' he mumbled under his breath, 'soon they'll want next of kin too.. . . 'Blimey,' they do too!' Dave thought of putting his ex-wife down, (blissfully unaware of his Freudian slip), as she was the closest he'd got left in life. He thought again and simply wrote, *Not Applicable*. 'That'll do them, it's only a room for the night, not as if I'm signing away my life,' he snorted a little drunken laugh.

A combination of moor-weary legs and the local brew contrived to make standing more of a struggle than he'd thought it would be. Success in standing drew a little smile of achievement to Dave's face and he wandered slowly across to the bar with his registration form in hand.

'There you are my dear. Shall I pay up front, and will there be a breakfast for me in the morning?' Dave inquired. Not waiting for an answer, Dave continued, 'Lovely stew that, tasty meat in it. Where does the pub get its supplies? Local farmer?'

The pretty one was studying the registration form intently and only half heard his questions. . . 'No need to pay until morning sir. Breakfast is full English with local sausages, from seven thirty onwards here in the bar. Oh, and the meat supply is one of our Chef's greatest secrets along with his preparation methods. . . but between you and me, I reckons there's a lot of cider goes along with it.'

'Betty will show you to your room sir, 'Betty! Show the gentleman to his room please,' have a lovely stay sir, sleep well.' She smiled her lovely smile again.

Betty, roughly prodding his arm, disturbed his day dream, 'This way sir.'

Ducking to miss even more beams and low doorways Dave followed Betty along poorly lit little corridors adorned by dusty old hunting-scene paintings and the occasional chest of drawers or dresser. As they reached some rickety old stairs, lit only by a lamp in a small curtainless window at the end of the hallway, Betty stopped, she opened a dark cupboard under the stairs and said, 'You can leave your walking gear in here sir if you like, it's what most other folk do.'

Dave peered into the shadows to see heaps of walking gear, boots, sticks, rucksacks. . . 'There's a lot of stuff in here Betty, whose is it?' Dave asked.

'Oh, it's just things that mostly them walkers must have forgot to take when they'm leaving Sir. Your things will be quite safe in there, but if you'm be afeared sir you can take it to your room, it's just that this is where the others seem to have left their stuff, that's all.'

Dave, any trust he'd had in the past having all but been beaten out of him, chose to keep his gear, his life's possessions in fact, with him. Anyways, he'd secretly contrived a plan to wash some of it when he had his bath.

He had a chance, the chance to set off tomorrow with a clean slate as well as a clean T shirt, a chance for a proper new beginning.

Life encouragingly beckoned him with a smile at last.

The room was simple and comfortable enough, yet seemed furnished with things likely to have been there since the building was first occupied. It was one of three attic rooms at the back of the pub; Dave could barely see the grey quarry rock face through the small grubby rooftop window; he wiped a little grime off the glass with his sleeve. Thinking out loud he mumbled how he could just make out a Raven's nest, heaped with sticks on a high protected ledge. Dave wondered if the birds might roost there and in the morning he could observe them much closer than those he'd seen quartering the open moor where intelligence and years of experience had made them such a wary and elusive creature.

As Betty began to close the door and bid Dave goodnight she said, 'Great big fat birds they Ravens sir, they're always hanging about around the pub. . . give me the creeps they do. You'll be seeing them again sir, you needn't have no fear of that. . . well, I'll bid 'ee goodnight sir,' and the door closed behind her with the soft click of a time worn old Yale lock.

At least the pub had been modernised; although about thirty years before! However, it did have a proper bathroom and enjoying a good long soak with some of his clothes for company did him the world of good. In fact Dave drifted off quite peacefully in the warm bath, only to be woken by imagined footsteps creaking their way along the landing floorboards outside his room. Though it initially startled him he was too tired to be bothered and was in any event still under the delusional influence of the mind numbing local brew he'd supped so rashly. He settled into the old sprung bed, pulled the too short blankets up to his chest and wondered what, if anything, the morrow might bring about.

Comforted by the good food and drink, the hot bath and the fatigue of worthy effort, Dave soon fell into a deep sleep. Normally he would wake frequently and mull over the many thought-provoking, and oft times disturbing, dreams that broke into his mind like the unwanted robbers of peace they were, but not this night, this night was for the sleep of the dead - unwaking and unknown.

**

The sound of a nearby Raven's call, karronk, karronk, brought Dave slowly out of a disorienting slumber and an almost amusing struggle to remember where he was. Slowly it all came back to him and then he dressed quickly in a clean T shirt that was now only slightly damp after a night on the bathroom towel rail, 'it'll soon dry on my back,' he thought as he tried to find his way back to the bar for breakfast. As Dave passed by the under-stairs cupboard he briefly shivered as if a chill had all of a sudden engulfed him, he put it down to his own silliness of wearing damp clothes to dry them off. 'Dozy burke,' he privately admonished himself. 'When will you ever learn?'

The bar was as though he'd never left it, everything in its place, even the pretty one was there with a smile for him. 'Morning to you sir, hope you slept well. Would you like tea or coffee with your breakfast? Juice and cereals are over there by your usual table,' she said with Summer in her voice.

'My usual table eh?' Dave thought, 'It's a long time since I felt I was at home and welcome. . . lovely, this is the life for sure. I wonder why I didn't do this earlier?' Dave selected a 'hair of the dog' apple juice and sat by his window, gazing out on a bright new day, the Sun already gently warming a strip of autumn road outside.

'I might go left this time old chap,' he said to another Dave, somewhere deep inside himself.

'Yes, why not? Let's see the village Betty spoke of,' came an amenable reply.

When the breakfast arrived, Dave had serious doubts about being able to finish it.

'Mind the plate - it be very hot sir,' said the pretty one. 'We're not short on meat here and I asked the Chef to pop some extra of the special sausages on for you. Chef's compliments and he's given you four of the little beauties - now that'll set you up fine for the day sir.'

Dave had other thoughts. Four substantial sausages along with all the other breakfast items wouldn't set him up, it would probably set him back, and one of his other thought was how much he would miss that pretty smile. 'You can always come back old chap, you can always come back; there's nothing to stop you now. We are free at last. . .' again he was speaking silently to the converted, the inner self that he was only now beginning to rediscover.

Breakfast finally done and all washed, gear packed and bill paid in cash according to the pub's preferred and only method,

Dave turned grudgingly towards the pub door and the beckoning outside world; he'd found a place that fulfilled his long search for happiness and he was reluctant to let it go.

'Damn it all to blazes,' Dave cursed as he suddenly became aware of the big silent fellow standing by the door again. Then loudly to the big fellow Dave joked, 'Do you stand there all night? Strewth, you made me jump; if I was older I'd be dead with a heart attack by now.' Dave smiled and found himself involuntarily returning one of those weird nods that the pub seemed to like so much.

The big fellow opened the door, 'Mind yer 'ead sir as ee goes; mind yer 'ead. Them beams can give ee a good whack sir, you won't know what's hit ee.'

Rucksack in hand Dave Baker, aged forty three, dreamily walked to the doorway, only hesitating to stoop and lower his head. . . the walker in him was about to begin a breathtaking new journey. . .

'We are the mapmakers of our own life.'

'There exists a moment in time and space where the world of opposites resides in fleeting but perfect harmony. If your mind is willing, it is beyond that gateway the great unknown beckons. You may cross the threshold many times never returning to the same place - nor the same you.'

'Nothing in this universe exists without an opposite. No sadness, no joy. No fear, no courage. No darkness, no light. No death, no life. No life, no death.'

'Despite your own belief of normality, somewhere beyond the gateway is an undeniable difference that patiently awaits your arrival.

Know this, we are only here, we only exist, because, somewhere out in the beyond, there is an opposite."

'*You are*, only because, *it is*.'

Edward Gaskell
publishers
DEVON